MARY

A STARLITE MYSTERY

THE STARLITE SUPERNATURAL MYSTERY SERIES

RAY & MICHELE FRASER

Hidden Door Press
Los Angeles, CA

Proofread by Paula Bothwell
www.pbproofreads.com

Cover design by Michele Fraser

The inspiration for this story is dedicated to all the survivors of Air France Flight 203.

CHAPTER 1
THE CRASH

The grinding sound of breaking metal became silent and there was a heavy scent of jet fuel throughout the cabin. Somehow, by the grace of God, I survived the crash.

The noise was deafening and pandemonium, caused by shock and fear, gripped the surviving passengers. Those who found themselves lucky to still be alive scrambled to exit the broken fuselage through missing windows or tears in the metal. At the rear of the plane, a burst of fire could be heard as sparks from broken electrical wires set the leaking jet fuel ablaze.

In the window seat across the aisle from me, a young girl of perhaps nine years of age sat still strapped into her seat. She was crying loudly, her voice rising above all the noise in the aircraft. The two seats which had been next to her and closest to the aisle, were missing.

As quickly as I could free myself from my seatbelt, I dashed across the aisle and loosened the girl's belt. In only a few moments, she was in my arms and we were climbing through a hole, into the cool, dark night.

A misting drizzle was falling, causing the grass to be wet. I slipped and fell flat on my back as I attempted to escape the crash scene. The weight of the girl falling on top of me caused me to momentarily lose my breath. I quickly regained my footing and began running away from the wreckage.

How far would be safe enough away? I wondered. There were horror stories about the fires that followed a plane crash. I didn't want to be a cinder in the middle of a field somewhere in Canada, so I kept running.

After what seemed to be about a hundred yards, I stopped and laid the young girl in the grass while I leaned on my knees and caught my breath. It surprised me how winded I was. I'm a hockey player, well-conditioned, and seldom out of breath, yet I was gasping now. The pressure of the moment was taking its toll.

After drawing in a few deep breaths, I began feeling better. I stood up and turned to look at the crash scene. The wreckage was totally engulfed with burning fuel. The fire stretched out in a winding pattern behind the jet like a jagged, flaming tail.

The site of the burning wreckage reminded me of a gigantic bonfire. Silhouettes darted around the twisted sections of the plane as rescue and fire crews busied themselves helping those in need, and doing their best to extinguish the raging fire. The support frames of the fuselage sections reached for the sky like the ribs of a slain animal.

I had this passing thought, *go back and help with the rescue effort*, but immediately dismissed the idea. Those who were helping with the crash scene were professionals. They didn't need my uneducated efforts getting in the way.

The young girl I had pulled from the plane lay on her side in the fetal position. I turned my attention to her.

"Are you all right?"

She nodded without comment.

The heat of the fire was noticeable even at our distance from it. The glare of the flames cast eerie, elongated shadows on the ground behind us.

For the first time since the plane skidded off the runway, there was a moment to reflect on what had occurred. We received no warning of any impending danger. Our approach to Toronto's Pearson International Airport had been normal. The landing, also uneventful, felt like any other I had experienced. Once the wheels had touched down, the pilots dutifully reversed the engines to slow the Airbus 330 to a taxiing speed. That's apparently when things went wrong. Instead of slowing, the aircraft continued down the runway and into the night.

At the end of the paved surface, the landing wheels struck the soft earth, and the plane lurched to the left and began sliding sideways. A short distance further, the left wing slammed into a chain-link fence, and the plane began tumbling, breaking into pieces. The remainder of the ride was a blur of screeching noises, sparks, and panic. I could hear the sounds of screaming voices above the breaking metal.

I sat on the ground, my legs crossed beneath me, watching the crews work around the still-flaming wreckage. Further down the runway, we could see the emergency lights of ambulances and rescue vehicles racing to assist those units already in position. They drove past the crash site to where several of us sat in small groups watching the unfolding events. The little girl sat up and assumed the same position that I was in. I looked at her while she stared blankly into the darkness.

"What's your name?" I asked.

"Mary," she whispered without looking at me.

"Are you hurt?"

Mary shook her head.

One of the emergency medical technicians exited a rescue vehicle near us and trotted in our direction.

"Anyone here injured?" she asked.

"I don't think so," I answered. "We're not bleeding and there don't appear to be any broken bones."

"Good," she said. "I'll be back in a few minutes." She left us and headed to a small group of people who appeared to be a family, sitting and lying to our left.

"Where are we?" Mary asked.

"We're in Toronto," I answered.

"How did we get here?"

"Are you sure you're okay?" I asked. "Don't you remember? We flew here on a jet."

Mary's look of confusion deepened. "What do you mean, flew?"

I pointed to the now smoldering wreckage. "You see that pile of metal?"

Mary nodded.

"We were on that. The plane crashed while landing. You do remember, don't you?"

Mary nodded slowly, and then also shook her head. She seemed totally confused. I thought to myself, *she's had a bump on the head and doesn't remember.*

"Did you hit your head?"

"No. I just remember you taking me off ..." Her voice trailed faintly. "I don't recall flying anywhere."

"We flew here from Boston. Where were you headed?"

"I'm from Massachusetts. Not Boston," she said.

"Boston is in Massachusetts. Are you from Boston?"

Again, Mary shook her head, staring at the fire. "No," she said.

"Do you know where you are from?" I asked.

Mary turned and looked at me for a moment. Then glanced back to the fire without answering.

Ironically, I didn't remember Mary getting on the plane either. I was sure there were passengers in the seats, because the aircraft was full, but for the life of me, I couldn't recall who or what they looked like.

"Were your parents on the plane with you?"

Again, a shake of her head, this time without her looking at me.

"Were you alone?"

Mary shrugged. "I don't know."

The EMS tech was back. The last name, Good, was displayed on her badge.

"No serious injuries?" she asked.

"Just some bumps and bruises," I answered. "I'm Jason Arnold. This is Mary. She says she's not hurt and was sitting across the aisle from me, alone. She says that her parents weren't on the plane, but also doesn't know if anyone else was with her."

"Did you hit your head, sweetie?" Good asked.

As before, Mary shook her head.

Technician Good looked at me questioningly. I shrugged. Mary's answers didn't seem logical, yet in truth, this whole event defied logic.

"Since you're both ambulatory, they'll be sending buses to take you to the terminal for debriefing and further medical evaluation. Do you think you can make it?"

I nodded. "Yeah, I think so. Mary, can you ride on a bus?"

Mary's stare continued to be blank, but she nodded slightly. I turned to the EMS tech.

"We'll be fine. Do you have a first name?"

The stern look softened. "Sarah. My name is Sarah."

"Okay. I'm not much on last names. I'm Jason Arnold. My friends call me Jay." We shook hands.

"Are you the Jason Arnold that's with the Red Wings?"

I offered a slight laugh. "Guilty as charged."

"Okay, then, Mr. Arnold, the buses will be here shortly. I'll be back to get you when they're ready."

I smiled at the concerned face. "Thank you, Sarah."

Back down the runway, the fire was now but a glow. Pockets of flames were being addressed by the same silhouettes that I had seen earlier. Everyone was moving slowly and deliberately. The firefighters were aggressively applying foam to the glowing embers. Trucks with huge halogen lights were taking up positions around the crash scene, their lights offering illumination to the grotesque pile of scrap metal that once was Air France Flight 203 out of Boston's Logan Airport.

Mary turned to look at me. "Did anyone die?"

"I don't know," I said, shaking my head. "It would seem hard to believe that everyone survived a crash like that."

"We did."

"Yes, we did, Mary," I answered. "We were very lucky."

I surveyed the space between where we were and the wreckage. Small groups of people stood, or sat, watching the progress of extinguishing the flames and rescuing any survivors. A lot of us had been lucky.

Down the runway, the headlights of several buses cut through the darkness. We were about to be transported to a safe area. I'd feel relieved to be away from the crash scene and able to call my wife.

"Jay, are you ready?" the voice said as the first bus lumbered to a site near where we sat. It was Sarah.

"We're ready," I answered, taking Mary's hand and pulling her to her feet.

We walked around the front of the bus to the door and fell in line with the other survivors who could make their way to the three buses.

"Do we need to follow these people?"

"Yes, Mary. They're going to take us to a safe place where it's warm, and we can find out about your parents."

Mary looked confused as we waited in line. She boarded the bus only after peering carefully and curiously inside. The light inside the bus was bright. Mary had preceded me and, for the first time, I got a clear view of what she was wearing.

She had on a full-length, dark-rust-colored dress that covered her from neck to ankle and completely down her arms to her wrists. The shoes she wore were more like boots and were more masculine than feminine. I wondered if she was Amish. Her attire looked as though it may have been a uniform of some kind.

Mary had short-cropped brown hair and hazel eyes. Her lips and cheeks were full and round. She looked like she could be anyone's nine-year-old daughter.

Our bus was about half full. We traveled slowly across the grassy area toward the lighted path of the runway. Once back on the paved surface, the diesel engine revved, and we picked up speed. We were finally on our way to the terminal. I looked forward to sitting on something solid, getting a drink of water, and calling Amy.

CHAPTER 2

DEBRIEFING

The terminal was well lit. Representatives from Air France stood inside and manned the doors to the lower-level facility. A large team of medical personnel also awaited our arrival. As the shock of the crash began wearing off, I felt a sharp pain in my neck. My right shoulder, which had been against the fuselage, also ached. I feared I had aggravated an injury that I suffered earlier in my hockey career.

Mary and I took seats in the blue plastic chairs. I was happy that she felt comfortable with me.

Sarah approached us. "Jason, what happened to your neck?"

When I put my hand there, it felt swollen. I shrugged. "I don't know. It hurts, though."

She turned to look for a doctor. "Let's get that checked out," she said, walking to where a well-dressed man was caring for a woman with a large knot on her forehead. As she spoke with him, she turned and pointed at us. The doctor acknowledged as he continued to work.

Sarah was back. "Dr. Eliett will examine you in a minute. Does anything else hurt?"

"Just my shoulder," I said. "I may have tweaked an old injury."

"Have him look at it. You may have broken something." Sarah turned to Mary. "Sweetie, do you hurt anywhere?"

The young girl slowly shook her brown hair. "Uh-uh. I just wanna go home."

Sarah looked at me before answering her. "You'll be going home in a little while. We just need to get in touch with your mom or dad. Someone will help us find them in a few minutes. Just make yourself comfortable. We'll have a snack for you soon."

"How many?" I asked.

Sarah turned to look at me and sighed. "Actually, we were very fortunate. We only have six people unaccounted for, out of more than three-hundred registered passengers. So far, there are a few serious injuries, but no fatalities."

I nodded. "We were lucky."

"Sir, may I speak with you?" A tall gentleman in an Air France shirt stood before us.

"Of course," I answered.

Sarah excused herself and went to assist others.

"I'm Henri LeBeau. I'm with Air France. We're trying to confirm registrations."

I spoke with Henri for approximately ten minutes, confirming my flight itinerary and role after the crash.

He looked at Mary. "Is this your daughter?"

"No," I answered. "She was a passenger on the plane. Her name is Mary, but I don't know her last name. She's from Massachusetts, but doesn't know what city. She said her parents weren't on the plane, but also didn't think she was alone."

The tall man sat down in an empty seat next to Mary.

"Do you know your last name, little one?"

Mary nodded, but said nothing.

Mr. LeBeau smiled. "Can you tell it to me?"

Mary whispered, "Parker."

"Good. So, your name is Mary Parker?"

Mary agreed.

"And, you're from Massachusetts?"

Again, she confirmed.

"From what city?"

Mary shrugged. "I don't know."

The questioning continued for several minutes. Mary was nine years old. She didn't know where her parents were and had no idea how she ended up on the plane. I found it very difficult to understand why she wasn't familiar with planes. Questions regarding her destination and relatives were all met with the same blank stare.

They had brought in trays of goodies and soft drinks and placed them on tables near the wall where we sat. I was very thirsty from the run and excitement. I figured Mary might be as well.

"Would you like something to eat?"

Mary smiled. "Yes, please."

"Great," I said, standing up. "Let's get a cookie and a drink."

Mary looked at the array with her hands behind her back. She appeared afraid to touch them or select one. I pointed to each style and explained what kind of cookie they were. After several shakes of her head, Mary selected a chocolate chip cookie. With her first bite, her eyes lit up.

"Is it good?" I asked.

She nodded vigorously.

I reached for a bottle of cola and twisted off the cap, closing it lightly so that she could open it herself. I handed her the bottle. She gave me a puzzled look. I opened one of my own and took a drink. She followed my example. Again, her face beamed.

"Let's sit down, Mary. My neck is hurting."

We returned to our seats and watched as others took their own light refreshments. I decided to see if I could gather more information from her.

Mary slowly ate her cookie, taking the smallest possible

bites. It was as though she were trying to make it last as long as possible. Sarah had been watching us from a distance. She walked by the snack table and brought Mary three more cookies.

Mary smiled broadly. "Thank you," she said, before carefully setting them on the napkin in her lap as if they were some valuable prizes.

Mary told me she had a brother named Arthur who was three years older. Their family lived in a small town with a water well in the center. Her father was a blacksmith. When I asked about what her mother did for a living, she cast me the most questioning look. She said her mother cooked, sewed, and only left the house to go to market.

I was concerned that Mary might be suffering from amnesia. It was also highly possible that she was in a state of shock from the accident, or had suffered a concussion.

"Mr. Arnold?" It was Mr. LeBeau.

"Yes," I answered.

He eyed Mary and then looked back at me.

"May I speak with you privately?"

"Sure," I said. "Mary, stay here for a minute. I'm just going over there to talk to Mr. LeBeau."

Mary nodded, still working on her second cookie.

I followed Henri until we were out of Mary's earshot.

He turned to face me. "Mr. Arnold, are you related to the young girl?"

"No. As I told you, she was just a passenger on the plane."

Mr. LeBeau shook his head. "No, sir, she was not on the plane. Everyone was accounted for. We checked all the boarding passes from Boston. There was no one on the plane with her name, nor anyone with the same last name. In short, there was no way she could have been on the plane. We checked with the people awaiting the plane's arrival here in Toronto. No one was expecting her. We've also asked our people in

Edmonton to do some preliminary investigations to see if it was possible that she was headed there. We think it's highly unlikely due to the fact that there's no record of her even being on the plane."

I stared at him for a minute. Was he kidding? What he was saying wasn't even remotely possible. I took her off the plane. She was strapped into a seat belt. I set her free.

"That's not possible," I said. "I took her off the plane. She was sitting in seat 27-A. There's got to be a mistake somewhere."

Again, he shook his head. "It cannot be a mistake. The only possibility is that someone brought her on the aircraft illegally."

Questions were forming in my mind. How did a nine-year-old girl get on a plane in Boston without being noticed? I knew from experience that with all the activity of getting a child on the plane, it was possible that her boarding pass could have been misplaced. The thought that she was on board illegally seemed illogical, especially since she occupied a seat on a full flight that no one else requested and with the extensive airline security in effect these days, it would be virtually impossible.

"They lost her boarding pass," I exclaimed.

Again, Henri shook his head. "We always do a passenger count. The girl was not on the plane."

"You realize that what you're saying is not possible," I asserted.

Henri's gaze never left my eyes. "So it would seem. I don't have an answer to our problem. I can only say that when the plane left Boston, Mary Parker was not on it."

I was at a loss. If Mary could not be identified and her family contacted, what would happen to her? I thought of my own daughters. The last thing that I'd want someone to do would be to leave one of them alone in a strange city. I personally couldn't do it to anyone else's daughter, and if I ever did, Amy would make me a eunuch.

"What's our next step?" I asked.

Henri shrugged. "I don't know. We'll have to leave it to the provincial authorities. They'll be here soon."

I went back to where Mary sat finishing her last cookie. Her cola was almost gone. She seemed content. I sat down beside her again.

"Mary, how did you get on the plane?"

Mary stopped eating and looked at me curiously. "What do you mean?" she asked.

I rephrased the question. "You were on the plane when it crashed. How did you get there? They don't have any record of you being on the plane."

"Mr. Jason, I don't understand what you ask of me. I don't know what you mean when you say plane."

It was obvious that Mary had incurred a bump on the head. There would be more time for conversation later. Dr. Eliett had returned.

The doctor's examination suggested that I may have re-injured my shoulder and that I more than likely had a severe case of whiplash. His examination of Mary indicated she had not suffered a bump on the head or physical trauma of any kind. She really didn't know what we were talking about.

My wife Amy called the airline after hearing about the crash. A young woman who represented Air France sought me out and acknowledged that they had informed her of my safety. That was a relief.

The events involving Mary had distracted me from even the most basic thoughts. I'd planned on calling Amy, but remembered my cell phone was in my carry-on bag. I was certain that it was nothing more than a piece of melted plastic, somewhere near the end of the runway.

People were beginning to leave. Those that needed medical attention were being escorted to ambulances for a ride to Toronto's University Hospital.

I wasn't sure what our next step would be, but my first priority was to get to a phone and call home.

Henri had made a public announcement requesting that we not give open statements to reporters or news personnel. He suggested that our safety and even our claims for injuries or damages could be affected by our loose conversation.

Sarah came from the ladies' room and walked to where Mary and I sat.

"Going home?" she asked.

I laughed. "If I am, I'm not flying. Dr. Eliett says I need to get my shoulder and my neck examined further. I'm thinking I may head back to the States and have the team doctor check me out. They're a little fussy about things like that."

"Perhaps you could have the Maple Leafs' doctors evaluate you before heading back."

Sarah had a good point. Teams in the National Hockey League tended to look after each other's players, and we were a lot closer to them than to my own doctors in Detroit. Still, it was only a five-hour ride home and there was Mary to take care of. I decided against the idea.

Sarah became serious. "They're debriefing all the able-bodied passengers and then arranging travel to their destinations. If you'd like, we can get you out of here. They'll give you a flight home, bus fare, or a train ticket."

I thought about the distance between Toronto and Detroit. I had driven it many times in my hockey career. It was a relatively short trip and seemed to be the most logical way to get home.

"I'd feel more comfortable being in control of my own transportation, if you follow me. Do you think they'll pay for a rental car?"

Sarah smiled. "I'm sure they will." She handed me a paper. "Write down your address and phone number and I'll make the arrangements for you."

She was back within minutes, and Henri was with her. He spoke first. "Because you're a public figure, we have approval from the provincial authorities and Air France for you to take Mary with you, considering she seems to be an American citizen. Honestly, they'd like to avoid any negative press about how she ended up on the plane without our knowledge. I've also made a call to customs, so you'll have no problems along the way."

Sarah added, "The rental pick up is just out the door and around the corner."

I nodded. "Thank you both for everything."

Sarah bent down and spoke to Mary, "Don't worry, all is as it should be." Then turned to me and stated, "Blessed be, Jason Arnold."

Mary asked, "Can I go home, too?"

CHAPTER 3

WHO IS MARY?

I was thinking of home and had temporarily forgotten about Mary.

"Don't worry," I said, "we'll get you home as soon as we can find out where that is."

Mary looked desperate. "I live in Massachusetts."

"Massachusetts is a big state. We need to find your mom and dad. Then we'll know where to send you. Can you remember what city you live in?"

Mary shook her head. "I just know that it has a big well in the middle of town. My father is a smithy. His name is Wilfred."

My mind assumed that locating Mary's father would be fairly easy. How many blacksmiths still worked in the modern day? I knew of one who made custom wrought-iron railings, furniture, and the like, but he was definitely a rarity.

My mind again entertained the idea that Mary was Amish. It would support the need for a blacksmith and perhaps even a well in the center of their village.

"Mary, are you Amish?" I asked.

Mary shook her head. "I don't think so. What does that mean?"

"Do you go to church?"

Again, Mary shook her head.

There went the Amish idea. I had no clue. I decided it was time to call Amy.

The phone had barely finished its first ring when she answered. "Hello?"

"Honey, I'm okay."

I heard some commotion in the background.

"It's Jason," she shouted.

Amy obviously had people over.

"Were you hurt?" she asked.

"No, I'm fine. Just a little shook up. Only a few minor bumps, but nothing's broken, and I'm not bleeding."

"We saw the pictures on the news," she said. "It's a miracle that anyone survived. You should have seen it. I was worried I'd lost you."

I laughed nervously. "Honey, I did see it—from the inside. It takes more than a little plane crash to kill me."

Amy was serious and actually fighting back tears. "Don't kid, Jason. It's not funny. We were worried sick."

We talked for a while, and I spoke with my daughters, Danielle, Jayna, and Kyla. They were definitely happy to hear from me and I was relieved to hear their voices. Amy came back on the phone.

"Honey," I said, "there's a little girl here who doesn't seem to remember where she lives. She said she's from Massachusetts, but doesn't know what city, and it doesn't appear that anyone is looking for her. They don't know how she got on the plane. If someone doesn't help her, the authorities will put her in a home until they find her family."

"What are you thinking?"

"Well," I said, "I was planning on renting a car to drive home. I thought I might bring her with me. At least she'd be in the US and we could work from our end to find her parents."

There was a long pause at the other end of the phone. "I don't know," Amy said. "Maybe we shouldn't get involved."

"She's only nine years old and scared. I thought the girls could help make her feel at home until we find her parents."

Danielle is 15, Jayna is 12, and Kyla's 10. They're very responsible for their ages and make friends easily. From a pragmatic point of view, it was a logical situation. However, I shared Amy's concern. These days, it's generally better not to get involved and let the authorities handle a situation like this, but Amy and I are both old school. We often ignore the present-day precautions to do the things we know are right.

"What if we can't find them?"

She had a point. What if we couldn't find her parents? The thought was reasonable, but illogical. The girl was on a fully loaded airplane that took off from Boston's Logan International Airport and was scheduled to land in Toronto. It was totally unreasonable to think she was there by accident or without someone noticing her. It was also ridiculous to think that no one would miss her.

"I hear what you're saying," I said. "But honey, that's not gonna happen. They have the Royal Canadian Mounted Police and the airlines looking for her parents. I suspect that when her plight hits the headlines, her friends and family will come forward. They said it might take a couple of days since she can't remember what city she is from, but I saved this little girl's life. It's not like she's a complete stranger."

Amy was quiet for a minute before speaking. "You're probably right, dear," she said. "I just don't want to get mixed up in something we shouldn't. You know what I mean?"

I knew what she meant. We didn't need to inherit anyone else's problems. We had enough of our own.

"It will only be for a few days. If we can't find her folks in a week, we'll take her to Massachusetts and let them help her. Agreed?"

Amy laughed. "Whatever you say. She can help us with the food drive on Saturday. That will give her something interesting and worthwhile to do."

"Wonderful," I said. "I'll fix things up from this end and call you when I'm on my way. I love you."

I could hear the smile in Amy's voice. "I love you, too."

Getting the proper releases, agreements, and commitments to let Mary come with me took a while, so it surprised me how quickly Air France agreed to pay for my rental car. At long last, Mary Parker and I were in a rented Ford, driving down Highway 401 to Detroit.

"Have you ever been to Michigan?" I asked.

Mary shook her head. "Is it in Massachusetts?"

I laughed. "No, Michigan is a state like Massachusetts. It's on the Canadian border. I live in a city near Detroit. Have you ever heard of it?"

Again, Mary shook her head.

"It was nicknamed the Motor City because cars were originally manufactured there."

This time, Mary nodded slightly. I thought she understood.

We rode in silence for a while, with Mary watching the scenery as it sped by.

"Mr. Jason?"

"Yes."

"Can I ask a question?"

I laughed. "Sure. Fire away."

"How does this carriage go without horses?"

I almost ran off the road. I turned to look at her, she was serious, which made me nervous.

"This is a car, it has a motor. It doesn't need horses."

The perplexed look on her face deepened.

"With no horses or oxen, what makes it go? And how does it go so quickly? Horses can't even gallop this fast!"

Mary seemed confused.

"Haven't you ever ridden in a car before?"

"No," she said with a shake of her head. "I've never even seen a carriage like this before. I once saw the king's carriage, but only for a minute. They wouldn't let me get close to it." Mary gazed off into the distance as though remembering. "He had six of the finest horses. They were all white." Mary turned to face me and got very excited. "He had several horsemen who rode with him and an honor guard that protected him. It was the finest carriage I have ever seen—until this one. The queen would want to ride in this carriage," she said with a nod of confirmation.

My mind did a quick geography and government calculation. I didn't know of a country that still had a ruling king and queen. However, I wasn't familiar with all the European or Middle Eastern countries. Mary didn't look Middle Eastern.

"What king did you see?"

"King William, of course. What other king is there?"

I shrugged my shoulders and looked at the road ahead of me. We were nearing London, Ontario. It would be a good time to get something to eat and use the restroom. The road sign stated that there was a service plaza four kilometers ahead.

"Are you hungry?"

Mary nodded. "Can we have another sweet?"

She caught me a bit off guard. "A cookie?"

Her beautiful smile indicated I had understood correctly.

I laughed. "I have something better than a cookie. It's called a milkshake."

Mary had apparently sustained a head injury. For the moment, I didn't know what I was going to do about that. The doctor had determined that there was no injury, but he also hadn't done a CT scan, or EEG because she had no symptoms. One thing at a time. Amy's friend Linda was a nurse. She might have some insights. We'd be in Detroit in a few hours. I was certain she would be part of the welcoming committee.

The lights of the plaza burned brightly ahead of us, and the Ford was still about half full, so I pulled into the parking lot for the food court and found a spot near the door. The plaza wasn't crowded, but Mary's dress had people turning their heads.

"Do you need to use the restroom?"

Mary's look told me she didn't understand.

"Do you have to go to the lavatory?" I repeated.

Again, the look of puzzlement.

She must have amnesia, I thought. A twinge of panic set in.

We stood outside the restroom area for a moment. A few women came and went. Finally, the attendant walked over to us.

"Can I help you, sir?" she asked.

I thought quickly. "This is my niece. Believe it or not, she's never seen a modern bathroom. I'm not sure she knows what to do. Could you please take her in?"

"Of course. Come with me. I'll take care of you."

"Mary, go with the lady. She'll show you the restroom."

They disappeared around the corner and I dashed into the men's room to take care of business. I was waiting for them when they came out. Mary was laughing.

"No problem," the attendant said. "Mary thinks the king and queen would like such a fine loo for their castle."

Mary jumped in quickly. "I feel better. I had to piss very badly. Now, I'm hungry."

I was surprised at Mary's language but didn't give it too much attention because of all the other events that had occurred since our meeting. There was certainly something amiss.

Our next stop was the burger counter. I got Mary a cheeseburger, french fries, and a chocolate shake. We took seats at the small round table near the window. I opened her sandwich wrapper and put a straw in her shake.

She stared at me.

I unwrapped my burger and took a bite, showing extreme

pleasure as I ate. Mary followed suit. Her smile revealed she was enjoying her food.

I followed my burger bite with a french fry. Again, she mimicked my lead.

"What are these?" she asked, holding a fry in the air.

I replied. "It's a french fry. Did you like it?"

Mary nodded. "Yes, but how did we get it from France?"

"We didn't get it from France. It was originally a French creation and now we make our own here. They're made from potatoes."

She ate a couple more fries and then said, "I'm thirsty."

"Have a drink of your shake. You'll like that."

Mary picked up the cup with the straw through the lid and tipped it upside down, thinking that the liquid would run down through the straw. I laughed.

"No, suck through the straw." I gave her a demonstration.

Mary followed suit, and as soon as she tasted the shake, she looked at me in delight.

"It's called a milkshake. Do you like it?"

Her eyes lit as she nodded with approval.

The remainder of the meal was quiet. After we threw the paper in the trash, we walked towards the door.

"Must we ride in the carriage again?"

"Only for a couple more hours," I answered. "We'll be home soon."

Just before we left the building, we passed a large map on the wall. It was complete with a *You Are Here* arrow. We stopped in front of it.

CHAPTER 4

HOME AT LAST

"Look, Mary. This is a map of Canada. The arrow points to where we are right now." I put my finger on Toronto. "This is where we started a few hours ago." Then I pointed to the map of Michigan. "This is where we're headed. See? We only have a short distance left."

Mary looked confused. "How did we get there?" she asked, pointing to Toronto.

"We flew on the plane. Don't you remember?"

She slowly shook her head, whispering, "No."

I decided this was probably not the best time to jog her memory about the plane and our crash. It would be better to discuss it when I was home with feminine reinforcements.

Soon after we got back on the highway, Mary fell asleep and didn't stir until we drove across the Ambassador Bridge which connected Windsor, Ontario and Detroit, Michigan.

Our stay at the customs booth was brief. The agent recognized my name and was extremely supportive when he found out we had survived the crash.

"It must have been quite an experience," he said.

I smiled. "Not something you'd want to do more than once

in a lifetime. We were very lucky."

Mary awoke long enough to get through customs, but once we had resumed our drive, she again fell asleep.

The Fisher Freeway was clear of traffic at five in the morning. We made good time and were soon exiting onto Sheldon Road in Plymouth Township. I would be extremely happy to be home.

I turned the Ford onto Capri Drive. *Only blocks from home*, I thought. The trauma of the day's events and the anticipation of seeing and holding my wife and girls rose to the surface. Tears streamed down my cheeks. For the moment, Mary's situation took a back seat to my impending reunion.

I brushed the tears from my face lest Amy see that I was shaken. There would be time for revealing my true emotions later. For now, I wanted her to feel the calm self-assurance that I was alive and well.

My driveway was full of cars, and literally every light in the house was on. I pulled into a vacant spot in front of the neighbor's house and nudged Mary.

"We're home. Wake up."

Mary stirred slowly and opened her eyes. "Will I see my mama?" she asked, not yet quite awake.

"No, not yet, we're at my house. We'll start trying to find your mother in the morning. Today, we're going to meet my wife and daughters. They're waiting to meet you."

Before we got out of the car, Amy spotted us and everyone came outside. She ran to me and we shared a warm embrace. I felt her tears on my neck and squeezed her tighter. God, how I loved her.

My girls stood patiently waiting. I opened my embrace and circled all three of them in my arms. They hugged me tightly. I had forgotten how sore my neck was, but hockey players are used to pain. I closed my eyes and enjoyed the love of my princesses.

Amy walked over to Mary and held her hands, she was getting the Arnold welcome. My sister-in-law, Heather, gave me a cursory hug.

"Are you okay?" she asked.

I nodded. "Yeah. I've got one hell of a stiff neck and my shoulder hurts, but I think I'll live."

Heather shook her head and then reached over to touch the side of my neck. "You need to get that checked, Jason. I don't like the way the muscle looks. You may have a tear in there."

When I slowly swiveled my neck around, it hurt. "I'll go to the hospital after I get some sleep and call Dr. Brandt to be sure he'll be there when I arrive. I don't want anyone screwing around with it. He'll check my shoulder, too."

Amy's sister, Heather, smiled. "Do me a favor. Don't let him find anything wrong. I'm not sure Amy could handle it. She almost had a nervous breakdown when she heard about the crash. They actually filmed it from the control tower. Then they showed it over and over on the news. We finally had to shut it off. When we found out there were survivors, she said, 'I'm making one phone call, then driving to Toronto.' She was totally flipped out."

Amy and I had always had a special relationship. We were on the same frequency almost from the moment we met. It took me a while to realize what we had, but once I did, it was a love like no other. After all this time, my feelings still continue to grow deeper each day.

I spent the next several minutes shaking hands with other well-wishers. It touched my heart to know that so many people cared.

We made our way back into the house. Some of the neighbors were unaware of what was transpiring, and we saw several porch lights go on as people questioned the outside activity.

"Channel 2 called," my brother Roger said. "They wanted to

know if we'd heard any news from you. I told them no. God, they're like vultures."

"Thanks, bro," I began. "I'd like to take a moment to introduce you all to a very special young lady. This is Mary Parker. She was on the plane with me when it crashed. I helped her to safety. She's going to be with us for a couple of days until we can find her parents. She's originally from Massachusetts."

Mary was approximately the same size as Kyla, except she was a tad thinner. I figured my daughter might have some fashionable clothes Mary could wear. That would be a project we could address after we'd rested a while. Everyone extended a greeting to Mary. She was quietly gracious to those who spoke to her. She appeared to be a respectful child.

I had recounted the crash experience a number of times. My family and friends were equally tired after having been up for nearly a full day. It was obvious I was safe and sound, at least for the moment.

Roger took the liberty of letting friends and family know that we wouldn't be accepting calls or visits till after three o'clock in the afternoon.

"Do you have a loo? I need to piss," Mary said.

Amy looked at me and then back at Mary. "Sorry, piss is a word we don't use in public. Do you need to go to the bathroom?"

"Is that a loo?" she asked.

I interceded, looking at them. "Yes, it is. Here, we call the loo a bathroom." I reminded Mary again it would be like the one she used in the rest area.

Mary looked at me as if I told her she had landed on a different planet.

I turned to Danielle. "Will you take her to the bathroom, show her how it all works, and then get her a nightgown to sleep in?"

Now it was Danielle's turn to stare. I gave her the *just do it* look, and she said, "Come on, Mary. We'll get you ready for bed."

All the girls disappeared upstairs to take care of Mary's needs.

When they were out of earshot, Amy spoke softly, "Jason, where the heck is she from?"

"No idea. I thought she was from Boston, but she said her dad is a smithy and they live in a town with a deep well in the center. I thought she was Amish, but she doesn't practice religion. So, there went that idea."

"She seems like she's from another country—like Russia or something," Amy said. "Did you see the dress she was wearing?"

I nodded. "There are several things that seem unusual to me. She talked about carriages, horses, oxen, and a king and queen. Plus, she was totally flabbergasted by the car and couldn't remember how she got on the plane. She had no clue why she was in Toronto. In fact, she didn't even know where it was."

Jayna called from upstairs, "Mom," drawing the word out into three syllables.

Amy looked at me and headed for the girls.

I was extremely tired. Everyone was leaving. I shook hands all around and gave hugs where appropriate. Soon, only Roger and I remained.

"You'd better get some sleep yourself," I offered.

Roger laughed. "No way. You need somebody to run interference while you and your family get some rest. I'll nap on the couch if I get tired. When you get up, I'll split and you can handle your own problems for a while."

I smiled. "Okay, you win. I'm headed for bed."

I started up the stairs and heard Amy talking to the girls.

"It's fine. It's just a tattoo. Different people have different customs. Don't worry about it." Amy came out of the bathroom just as I was reaching the top of the steps.

"What's up?" I asked.

Amy looked exasperated. "Oh, it's no big deal. Mary has a tattoo on her chest. It's a letter and a cross. Jayna got Mary to take a shower and when she saw it, she freaked out a bit."

"She's a little young to have a tattoo, don't you think?"

Amy agreed. "Here in the States, yes. But, Jason, we don't know where she came from. It might be a family emblem or tradition."

"I've heard of people hanging plaques on their walls, but not tattooing their kids." I ran my hand through my hair, wincing at the pain in my shoulder and neck. "You may be right. Guess we'll figure it out when we find her folks."

My sleep was restless, and I was startled awake more than once. I was sweating and my shoulder ached the longer I lay on it. When I looked at the clock, it was nearly 2:00. Amy lay sleeping beside me. I snuggled close, kissing her first on the neck and then on the top of her head. I always loved the way her hair smelled.

My mind was racing. Mary's situation had been filed into the back reaches of my thoughts. The close call was a haunting experience. I pictured Amy and the girls. *What if I never saw them again?* My heart sank at the thought. *Thank you, God, for letting me live.* I pulled Amy closer, wrapping my arm around her middle. She snuggled back against me.

Who was Mary? Kids just didn't get on planes alone. She had to have a family connection somewhere. I was also concerned about why she was so unfamiliar with our modern amenities. Even in the less developed countries of the world, they had toilets and cars. Besides, she said she was from Massachusetts. That's hardly a third-world area. Too many questions and not enough answers.

Amy shifted and rolled onto her back. I leaned over and kissed her softly on the lips. Her arm came up and circled my chest, drawing me closer to her. The answers would have to wait.

CHAPTER 5
THE MEDIA

I t was difficult to leave the warmth of our bed and Amy's caress, especially after the closeness we had just shared, but staying in bed wasn't an option. We both knew time was fleeting, and I needed to see the doctor.

Getting dressed was a challenge. Every muscle seemed to ache. Thankfully, Amy helped where she could and soon the smell of coffee drew me to the kitchen.

"Sleeping Beauty arises," Roger said.

I laughed. "Barely," I answered. "I feel like I was in a plane crash."

Roger looked at my neck. "Man, you need to see the doc. He had an opening at four, so I got you an appointment."

Roger was right. When Amy and I took a shower, she noticed that the right side of my neck and shoulder were bruised almost to the waist. I couldn't lift my right arm to wash my hair. The bruise wrapped all the way around to my abdomen. Something was definitely wrong. I wondered if I had cracked a rib or two. A preliminary examination hadn't seemed to indicate anything broken, but it had been incomplete. After some x-rays, hopefully Dr. Brandt would figure it out.

"I'll be there," I said, checking the time.

I had about forty minutes before the appointment. That would give me time for a snack and a brief talk with Mary. I wanted to get started on finding her family as soon as possible.

The noise upstairs told me that the girls were also up and around. There was laughing, toilet flushing, running water, and more laughing. It appeared that the girls and Mary were getting along just fine. After approximately fifteen minutes, there were footsteps on the stairs. The girls were joining the living world.

Kyla was first, then Danielle, followed by Jayna, and finally Mary. I stared in disbelief. Mary was wearing one of Kyla's outfits. She had on pants and a pull-over top. She looked different.

"She didn't want to wear the pants," Danielle said. "She said women don't wear pants."

Mary had pulled her shoulder-length brown hair back into a bun. She looked much older.

Amy had made sandwiches for everyone. Mary had no hesitation in digging into the feast. She readily accepted the cola, and when we had all eaten, she asked if we had a sweet. Fortunately, chocolate chip cookies were a staple in our household. She was halfway through her second cookie when I broke the silence.

"Mary, have you been able to remember what city you lived in?"

Mary shook her head. "No, but my father is the smithy. You'll be able to find him."

"What's your mother's name?" I asked.

"Christina," Mary answered.

Her parents' names had an old-world ring to them. Was it possible that they were originally from Europe?

"Has your family lived in Massachusetts all your life?"

Mary nodded. "Uh-huh. We lived in a smaller town for a

while before we moved to the city with the well so my father could find work."

"You said that you didn't practice a religion, but what does your family believe in?"

Mary answered. "I think we're Roman Catholic, but I've never been to church. The people in the town were not very friendly with us. I think that's why my father decided to send me away."

Mary's statements didn't seem to be realistic. How could she be Catholic, without ever going to church? I remembered she had talked about a king, so I approached the topic.

"Mary, you said there was a King William who ruled your country. What was his queen's name?"

She beamed. "Mary. Just like me. I was named after Queen Mary the First. The king's queen is Mary the Second. I sometimes pretend that I am her." Mary became serious and slowly waved her hand in a circular, horizontal arc. "More food for everyone," she said. "No more sacrifices to the king. All the slaves will be freed." The smile returned to her face. "Don't you think I'd make a good queen?" she asked.

I nodded. "Yes, Mary. You'd make a wonderful queen, but for now, Your Majesty, I must bid you adieu."

Even though we haven't had any breakthroughs, my research would have to be put on hold. "I'm off to the doctor." I turned to Amy. "Do you all want to come?"

She shook her head. "No. I've got stuff to do. I think it would be best if Mary was kept out of the limelight for a while, anyway. Just be careful."

"I will," I said. "I'll be back in an hour or so."

Three cracked ribs, Dr. Brandt had said, plus severe contusions in the muscles of my neck, side and back, but nothing was broken or re-injured in my shoulder. "Take two of these tonight, and then one every four hours thereafter," he said, handing me the anti-inflammatory pills. "And don't drive after you take these."

The pain was intense, so I was eager to get home and take the meds.

Rush hour was in full gear, and traffic was backing up. It would take longer to get home than I had hoped. I opted to swing by Cellular and More and pick up a new phone on the way.

My friend Ron came out of his office and greeted me. "Good to see you."

"Better seen than viewed," I quickly replied.

Ron chuckled and then said seriously, "Mom said you were on that plane. We all thought you were a goner."

Ron's mother and I had been friends for many years. She was born in Canada, and they both shared dual US and Canadian citizenship.

I sighed. "I thought I was a goner too," I said. "Actually, you don't have time to think. You just kinda roll with it, and hope you have the chance to get out. Thank goodness everyone did."

"That's amazing. I'll let Mom know you stopped in."

With my new phone in hand, I called Amy to tell her I was on my way.

"Get here as soon as you can. They're crawling through the bushes to try and talk to Mary. Roger left right after you did, so I'm trying to fight them off by myself. I called Heather and asked her to come and help. She's on her way. There's also something I want to show you when you get here. I'm not sure I believe it, but it's another piece of the puzzle."

"What is it?"

"Not on the phone. This one you've gotta see."

My curiosity peaked. I pressed a little harder on the gas.

Just as Amy said, reporters filled the street and sidewalk in front of our house. I guess a plane crash with survivors was a big deal. Plus, a situation like Mary's had never happened before. I certainly didn't want the media making a spectacle of her while we were still trying to locate her family. I keyed the garage door opener, driving slowly so the people could get out of my way. Once inside, I hit the controller again, and the door closed behind me, locking the news cameras out.

"Finally," Heather said. "Jason, can you get these people off the porch?"

I decided that the easiest way to get rid of them would be to go out and talk to them. I'd give them some information with a stern assertion that they needed to keep their buns off my property. I did not like to have my privacy invaded.

The interview was mostly superficial: How did I feel? Did I see anyone else getting out? What was it like when it started? These were addressed easily enough. I thought I could return to the sanctity of my home without a confrontation until one of the lady reporters spoke.

"Mr. Arnold, I understand you saved a little girl's life, and that she is now staying with you. Why is that?"

I took a deep breath. The last thing I wanted to do was to create a circus around Mary's existence, but the media might be of help.

"Yes, that's true. There was a young American girl on the plane named Mary Parker. I was able to rescue her from the crash. My wife and I invited her to our home until her family could be notified. The airline authorities were having some difficulty locating them. We felt she would be better off in the US and Air France officials and Canadian authorities agreed. Mary is nine years old and from Massachusetts."

All the reporters pressed forward. There were shouts, "When can we talk to her? Can we get a picture of her? What do you know about her?"

Enough was enough.

"I will be working with the authorities on this matter, starting first thing in the morning. On their advice and with the guidance of my attorney, we will release more information as soon as possible. Now, if you don't mind, I need to get some rest and spend time with my family. I would appreciate your respect, so please do not contact me, or come onto my property unless you're invited to do so. If you're unable to honor my request, I will take whatever action is necessary to secure our safety and tranquility."

I closed the front door and turned to Amy. She was shaking her head.

"They haven't moved an inch, Jay. I think we're trapped in our own home."

"No, honey, I don't think so," I answered. "I'll call Larry and have him chase them away. Besides, I want the police to begin searching for her parents."

Larry Parish was a good friend and long-time police detective with Plymouth Township. He would have all the resources we needed, and the authority to use them. He could also help us keep our peace and solitude.

"I'll be damned," Heather said. "They don't waste any time, do they?"

The television was showing the interview which I had just completed. A reporter named Candice Sinclair was recounting our statements. She seemed sincerely interested in Mary's well-being. Maybe she would be an ally. I figured it would be better to wait until after I talked to Larry to call her.

"Where are the girls?" I asked.

"Upstairs, watching the tube. Mary acts like she's never seen a television before," Amy said. "Then again, she acts like there are a lot of things she has never seen before."

I agreed. "I get the feeling that she's not being honest about her background. Either that, or she truly doesn't remember. I believe that shock could do that."

"Mind if I go up and sit with them?" Heather asked.

I shook my head. "Not at all. Anything you can pick up will definitely help."

Heather started for the stairs. Amy held up her finger, suggesting that she wait a minute.

"There's something I want to show you guys," she said, leaving the room. She was back in a flash. "Here, look at this."

CHAPTER 6

HER DRESS

Amy handed me Mary's dress. I looked at it.

"Yeah. So what? It's a dress," I said.

"Look at the hem, Jason. It was all done by hand. In fact, the dress is completely hand sewn."

I examined the stitching, turned it inside out, and looked at the seams. Clearly, they hadn't used a sewing machine. Plus, the edges were rough where the fabric was pieced together. It looked like someone needed their scissors sharpened.

I took a deep breath and exhaled. "Well, it seems like wherever she's from, they lack the conveniences of modern technology. I also notice there's no label in the dress. She obviously didn't get it at a department store."

After I checked the dress, I handed it to Heather. She followed my lead, scrutinizing not only the seams, but the cutting lines and stitching.

The phone rang. "I'll get it," I said, readying myself for a reporter's onslaught. To my surprise, it was Larry Parish.

"What are you, psychic or something?" I asked with a laugh.

Larry replied. "I smell trouble, Jay. How are you?"

"I'm okay, but you know I have a minor situation."

"I've heard. Need some help?"

"Actually, yes," I said. "I was just going to call you. This is getting a little weird."

"I can be there in ten minutes. Does Amy still make her specialty coffee?"

"For you, any time. We'll see you when you get here."

"Was it Larry?" Amy inquired.

I nodded. "Yeah. He's on his way. He wants some coffee. Got anything brewing?"

Amy shook her head and smiled. "I'll fix something up for him."

Danielle came downstairs, passing Heather, who was on her way up.

"Can we eat?" she asked.

"Order a couple of pizzas," I said. "See what Mary wants on hers and then get one for us."

"Can we get some bread and a salad?" Danielle asked.

"Yes, dear. Order whatever you want. Just make sure we get some pop."

Danielle disappeared into the kitchen to check on the soft drinks. I heard the refrigerator close, and then her footsteps going upstairs. She was very responsible. I trusted her to get things right and place the order. It would be about 30 minutes before we'd be able to eat. Hopefully, Larry would be here to join us.

With his help, I wanted to get down to some direct questioning. I was planning on spending the evening online trying to research some information to help us find Mary's family.

"Jason, do you really think you'll be able to find her parents?" Amy asked.

"Yeah, I think so," I responded with a nod. "If she were older and on her own, it would probably be harder, but a nine-year-old has to be living with someone. We'll find her family—wherever they are."

Danielle was back. She had a weird expression on her face.

"What's up, Dani?"

"We have a problem."

I sighed. "What, now?"

"Dad, she's weird."

"Describe weird for me," I answered, somewhat exasperated.

Danielle sat down on the couch. "Okay. Like, she doesn't know what a shower is, doesn't know how to flush a toilet, she's never seen a toothbrush, she asked how we got the straw into our mattresses, she's never seen a TV, she's got a tattoo on her chest, and get this, she's never heard of a pizza! I told her it was an Italian dish, and she asked me when we started trading with the Italians. She freaks me out."

Amy had a perplexed look on her face. "Jason?"

I tried to remain as calm as I could, looking directly into her eyes. "Yes, honey?"

Amy was frustrated. "Don't you *yes, honey*, me. What's going on?"

"Hopefully, we're going to find out," I replied. "This is not your usual Arnold family issue. I agree that things with Mary don't seem normal, but let's not be too hard on her. Larry will help us figure it out. He's an expert at this." I turned to Danielle. "Did you order the pizza?"

"Yeah. They said it would be here in half an hour. I ordered an extra-large ham and cheese for us, a super deluxe for you, cheese bread, a large salad, and two bottles of pop. It's like $66.00 something."

I shook my head. "Did they have anything on the menu that you didn't order?"

Danielle cast me a confused look. "Only wings. Did you want me to order some of those?"

"No, Dani," I said. "You did good." I turned to Amy and smiled. "You got any cash?" It's no wonder so many parents consider bankruptcy. Feeding the flock is expensive.

The doorbell rang. It was Larry. The pizza wouldn't be far behind.

We shared greetings and family updates.

"Did you have your neck checked?" he asked after he saw the bruising.

I replied, "It's only a superficial wound, just hyper-extended muscles. The doc said I couldn't watch tennis matches for a while. Other than that, I'll be okay."

The doorbell rang again. It was time to eat.

Amy called upstairs, and immediately you could tell the girls and Heather would be joining us.

The noise coming down indicated they were heading for the food at a full run. "Don't fall," I whispered to myself.

They threw open the lids on the pizza boxes, and everyone began digging in. I should say, everyone except Mary. She stood back and watched everyone place the triangular slices on their plates. She did nothing.

"Go ahead and eat," I said. "Haven't you ever had pizza before?"

Mary shook her head. "What is this?"

I smiled. "It's made with bread dough, tomato sauce, and cheese. It's delicious."

She frowned.

Amy was looking at me as if she'd seen a ghost. Her attitude was simply, *fix it, Jason.* I acknowledged her look and tried my best.

"Mary, remember when we were coming here from Toronto and we had french fries?"

Mary nodded.

"Pizza, like french fries, is made in our country now. The Italians told us we could have the recipe—as the French did with their fried potatoes. They made this in America, and none of the ingredients are from Italy. Eat and enjoy."

Mary smiled. "Then it's accepted?" she asked.

"Perfectly okay," I answered. "Even your father would eat it."

She paused for a moment. "Do you know my father?"

Nice move, Jason, I thought. *Open mouth, insert foot.*

"Uh, no, but I know people like him. They'd eat the pizza. Besides, we have cola to drink with it."

Mary's eyes lit up with her smile. In a very short time, she had made a feast of the pizza, cheese bread, and salad. Her first bites were tentative, but soon she was laughing with the girls and enjoying the food.

I noticed Heather's unusually quiet demeanor.

"What's up?"

Heather just looked at me and shook her head. I looked at Amy. She had a puzzled look on her face.

"Do we need to talk?" I asked.

Heather nodded. "Later."

Larry spent a good deal of time after dinner making conversation with Mary. I told her exactly who he was and why he was asking the questions. He took her fingerprints and a digital photo to help with his search.

Larry asked Mary several questions, which confirmed that her father was a blacksmith, and her mother, a housewife and seamstress. She said that her brother did not attend school, but helped in the stables for scraps of food and vegetables. They had a large cat that everyone in the town loved. Midnight was the friend of everyone who visited her father's blacksmith shop.

Larry cast me a look of frustration. We were getting nowhere. After more than an hour of conversation, we were no further ahead than when we'd started.

"That's all for now, Mary," Larry said. "Thank you for your help."

After she left the room, he turned to me.

"I don't get it, Jay. She's so comfortable with her story, it's as if it were true. We'll run her prints through the system. I doubt there will be anything on file, but for now, it's all we've got. I'll also do a global name search. She had to be born somewhere."

Larry left with a wave. As I closed the door behind him, Amy was at my side.

"Do you think we should take her to the doctor?" she asked.

"She doesn't seem ill or injured," I answered. "Besides, I'm not sure if we should get involved in her medical care at this point. I'm gonna spend some time online. I want to see if I can come up with anything. Who knows, it may be easier than we think."

I wanted Amy to be comfortable with the situation, even though I wasn't entirely at peace with it myself. I hoped my research would produce a lead.

"Is Heather still upstairs?" I inquired.

Amy shook her head. "No, she had to leave. She left while you were with Larry. She said she would talk to you later. What do you think is on her mind?"

"Not sure, honey. You know how Heather is. Once she gets something in her head, she won't let it go. I'm sure she'll be in touch."

Heather was extremely opinionated. If she thought something was important, it was better to just listen and accept her point of view than to try and fight it or argue.

The girls had eaten their fill and sat in front of the TV watching a popular family show. As Amy had said earlier, Mary initially stared at the television like it was a work of magic. After a few minutes, she seemed to relax.

After reading Dr. Brandt's report, the Red Wings' coaching staff told me to stay at home for a few days. The timing was perfect, as it would allow me an opportunity to dig in and do some investigating. I headed for the computer.

The computer returned more than a thousand listings when I entered the name Parker into the search engine. *I'll never be able to evaluate them all*, I thought.

I took a chance and entered Mary Parker. Again, hundreds of listings. Of all the last names that Mary could have, why Parker? It was too common to make my search simple.

Next, I tried Wilford Parker, but nothing came up. My last effort was Christina Parker. I hit the enter key. Bingo, a match, 36356 Fine Road, Salem, Massachusetts 01970. I hit the print key and waited for the paper to slide out with the information. "At least it's a name," I muttered.

"Is everything okay? You're talking to yourself," Amy said.

I laughed. "You're right, I am. I got a name. It's the same as Mary's mother. Maybe it's her."

CHAPTER 7
PICTURES

Igrabbed the paper out of the printer, crossed my fingers, and reached for my phone.

I keyed the numbers in and paused. After a moment, I ended the call. Several thoughts rushed to my mind. Why Christina and not Wilford? Salem wasn't New York City, but it definitely wasn't wilderness either. Could they still have open wells in Salem? My mind told me no, but my heart was hoping for a miracle.

I cued up the Salem Chamber of Commerce website. They had a great deal of information regarding events and historic sites, but nothing about a village that might have been reconstructed to replicate a time long ago. I sat back in my computer chair and let out a deep sigh.

I reached for the phone again and dialed the number. After four rings, someone picked up.

"Hello?"

"Is this Christina Parker?"

"It is," the soft voice answered. "Who's calling?"

"Mrs. Parker, you don't know me, but my name is Jason Arnold. I'm calling you from Detroit, Michigan."

Over the next half hour, I explained everything that had happened. She saw the plane crash on the news and was amazed no one died. Unfortunately, she didn't know Mary and had no children of her own. There was a large family of Parkers in the area. No one she knew had a daughter named Mary.

"She may be a distant relative," she said. "Are you sure she's from Massachusetts?"

I nodded at my end of the phone. "She says she is, but she can't remember the city."

We finished the conversation, and I was about to hang up when I received an inspiration.

"Christina, would you mind if I came to Massachusetts and talked with you and some of the family members in person?"

"Of course not," she said. "Someone might have a clue. When are you coming?"

I jumped at the chance. "I'll be there tomorrow afternoon."

"Very well, then. I'll check around today to find out what people know and see if there's anyone you can meet with."

I hung up the phone and turned to Amy.

"I know," she said with her arms crossed. "You're going to Massachusetts. I'll make the reservations."

The girls and Mary seemed to be hitting it off quite well. I felt comfortable leaving her at home for a day or so while I did some research. Before I left, I wanted to take several photos of Mary. I needed some in the clothes I found her in, and a few more in everyday attire.

As soon as I got up in the morning, the anticipated plane flight, had me petrified.

Amy picked up on it when we were having breakfast. "You seem tense. Are you sure you want to do this?"

I laughed. "No, I'm not sure. My stomach is in knots, but if I don't, we may keep Mary away from her family longer than necessary. I'll be back the day after tomorrow."

"Why don't you call Larry before you go and see if he came up with anything?"

That's what I love about Amy. She covers all the details. I reached for the phone.

Larry's search was going nowhere. In fact, he had less information than I did. I filled him in and asked him to keep a watch on the house for a couple of days. He assured me he would.

The girls were stirring around upstairs. We could hear them talking loudly. It would be a typical morning in the Arnold household. After about thirty minutes of laughing, shouting, and squeals, the girls graced our presence. They all looked freshly washed and put together. Mary had her hair pulled back in a french braid. She looked very different from the girl I had pulled off the plane. She actually seemed like she was enjoying herself.

As I watched the girls mill about the kitchen fixing something to eat, I noticed something was different. I watched them as they fixed cereal, toaster waffles, and poured drinks. What was it? I chided myself for an overactive imagination. *Too much pressure in too short a time*, I thought.

When the girls were about half finished with their breakfast, I let Mary in on my plans for the day.

"I'm going to fly to Massachusetts and meet with a lady who has the same name as your mother. Hopefully, she'll be able to help me find your parents. Does the city of Salem ring a bell with you?"

Mary thought for a moment and then shook her head.

"No. Not really. Why is that where I live?"

I laughed. "Not sure, Mary. I'm trying to find out. If I have a few pictures of you to take with me, maybe someone will recognize you."

Mary stared at me as though I had been speaking to someone else.

I continued, "Let's take a few the way you're dressed now

and some with the dress you were wearing on the plane. That way, I can let people see you as you were on the day of the crash."

Again, the blank stare.

When we finished breakfast, I asked the girls to gather around so I could take a group picture. At least we'd have one for future memories. Things like this didn't happen often.

Mary was standing between Jayna and Kyla. Danielle stood to Jayna's left. As I looked through the camera's viewfinder, it hit me what was different. I clicked the pictures, then took several of Mary alone, and then asked her to go change clothes for a photo in her original outfit. The girls all screeched up the stairs to help.

Amy saw the puzzled look on my face. "What?" she inquired.

I shrugged. "Granted, I've had a couple of rough days and probably got a knock on the head, but something is going on."

"Like what?" she insisted.

"Okay, so call me crazy," I began, "but, if I remember correctly, Kyla was taller than Mary."

Amy returned my puzzled look.

"Yeah, so?"

"Look at these pictures."

I swiped the images back to the beginning and showed her the pictures of Mary standing next to Kyla. Mary was now nearly two inches taller than her. It's impossible. Just the day before, Kyla was taller.

"Shoes," Amy said. "It has to be the shoes."

I looked at the uncertainty on her face. She didn't believe it any more than I did.

"Right," I said.

Mary was back in her original outfit. She kinda looked like I had found her, yet now there was a noticeable difference. The hem of her dress was up off her shoes, and her sleeves were further away from her wrists. I took several photos, and the girls bolted upstairs again with Mary to change back into modern clothes.

Amy stood beside me as I reviewed the photos.

"Did you wash it in hot water?"

Amy shook her head. "No."

"You see it, too. Don't you?"

"Jason, it's not normal for anyone to grow that quickly. It had to be her shoes or something."

"That's why her dress—the one she was wearing when we arrived—doesn't fit her today, right?"

"What are you saying?" she countered.

"Honey, I don't know, but it appears Mary has grown about four inches in just a short time."

"That's not possible," Amy whispered.

"That's what I keep telling myself, too," I muttered.

The girls returned and came to look at the pictures. When I showed Mary, she slowly ran her fingers over the photograph.

"How did you do that?" she asked.

"Do what?"

"Take my image like that. Are you a painter?"

I laughed. "No. It's a photograph. The camera takes it digitally."

Mary's face looked like she'd seen a ghost.

Danielle quickly interjected, "Don't worry, Mary. You look fine."

Jayna added, "They turned out great."

"What time are you leaving?" Amy asked.

"Right after I use the bathroom. What are you guys going to do?"

"I'm taking the girls to the mall. Somehow, I think it's going to be an experience I will never forget."

"Call and tell me how that turns out," I exclaimed.

We shared a tender embrace and several kisses. I didn't want to let go of Amy. I was still apprehensive about leaving, but I knew it was something I had to do.

I took care of business, put my phone and the address information into my attaché case, and was out the door and on my way.

The airport wasn't crowded, but my nerves made me uneasy as I walked through the security area and down to my gate. It was still nearly an hour before I would board, so I stopped in the lounge and had a drink. I needed something to help take the edge off.

Unfortunately, I couldn't find any non-stop flights from Detroit to Boston. My only option was a two-hour layover in Chicago. I'll never understand why the airlines insist on flying in the wrong direction before they send you to the desired destination. What a waste of time, energy, and fuel. When I finally arrived at Logan International Airport, it would be nearly six hours later. Fortunately, Salem is only about twenty miles from Boston, so provided I didn't run into any traffic tie-ups, the drive would take fewer than thirty minutes.

I spent the layover having a bite to eat and a couple of shots of scotch on the rocks. As soon as the wheels left the ground in Chicago, the alcohol did what I had hoped it would do. I slept until I heard the flight attendant announce our impending arrival in Boston. It was just before five o'clock.

I felt no apprehension or anxiety about meeting Mrs. Parker until I turned my rental car onto Highway One and headed for Salem. I wondered what Christina would be like. Old? Young? I took a deep breath and sighed. I'd soon find out.

The GPS led me right to Fine Road and her residence without any issues.

Christina Parker's home was a one-story ranch that looked like it was probably built in the 1920s. It was set back off the street by approximately twenty-five yards and had a large screened-in front porch. Flowers lined the walkway and the front edge of the house. It was a comfortable looking abode.

By the time I had reached the door of the porch, a small, gray-haired woman stood waiting for me.

"Mr. Arnold?" she asked with a slight waver in her voice.

"I am," I replied. "You must be Christina Parker."

I was invited in and offered a seat on the porch.

"Would you like some lemonade?" she asked.

I thanked her and said that I would. She disappeared into the house.

CHAPTER 8

THE SEARCH

Christina returned. The lemonade was freshly squeezed and properly sweetened.

After relating the events of the past few days and learning that Christina had been a widow for more than forty years, we moved on to discussing the possible family ties that Mary might have with the other Parker families in the area.

"I'm quite active in the chamber of commerce here in Salem and, to my knowledge, no one has a daughter or granddaughter named Mary."

"I do have some pictures," I said. "Would you care to look at them? It's possible she suffered some form of amnesia and can't remember her real name."

Christina pored over the pictures, adjusting her glasses as she did so.

After a long period of study, she shook her head. "I'm sorry, Mr. Arnold. I don't recognize her. She has the Parker eyes and her hairline is similar to other family members that I know, but ..." Her voice trailed off.

"I understand. I'll be here for another two days. Can you tell me where I might look to find more information?"

"Why, yes," she said. "I have a friend that works at the historical society. She may be able to help, especially since you have pictures." Christina thought for a moment. "Other friends of mine work at the library. Maybe they can offer some insights."

"I'll be staying at the Salem Motel," I said as I stood to leave. "Please give me a call if you come up with anything."

Christina had written her friend's name at the historical society on a piece of paper. With the contact info securely in my pocket, I headed down to Essex Street and the Salem Historical Society.

Much of downtown Salem reflected a time gone by. Buildings were restored, but kept the historical ambiance of yesteryear. The Salem Historical Society was no different. It was a two-story brownstone building that emulated a period long ago. A melodious chime signaled my entrance. A slender, middle-aged woman emerged from the doorway at the rear of the room.

She smiled. "May I help you?"

"Yes," I began. "I'm looking for Harriet."

"That's me," she declared. "You must be Mr. Arnold."

"I am," I replied. "Mrs. Parker said you might be able to help me."

"Yes, Christina called and said that you'd be coming. What can I do for you?"

I explained my dilemma and inability to make any progress in finding Mary's parents.

Harriet pursed her lips before answering. "Well, we have some archives here, but there are other places, with more sources. You mentioned Mary was nine years old."

"Yes, that's what she says, but the fact she can't remember what city she's from may be an indication that she doesn't honestly know. She seems to be around the same age as my ten-year-old daughter."

"Well, the records here date back approximately fifty years.

We mostly cater to the tourists, so if we don't have any luck, I can give you other places which may be able to help."

I quickly remembered Mary was adamant about her father's occupation. "Are there any working blacksmiths in Salem?"

"Yes," Harriet said, "but only one. His name is Peter Anthony. Unfortunately, he's elderly and has never been married. I doubt he could be related. I've known him most of my life and he's never had a close family."

"Well, I may want to chat with him while I'm here. If we can't find Mary's parents, I want to be certain that I don't leave any stone unturned."

Harriet didn't recognize Mary when I showed her the pictures. She immediately raised her eyebrows upon seeing the dress I had found her in, and exclaimed, "That's what she was wearing?"

When I acknowledged it was, she told me it resembled a style of dress from centuries ago. That's all I needed—more intrigue.

We reached a dead end. There was nothing in their archives that could place Mary or her parents. Before I left, Harriet gave me the address of the Salem Witch Museum. It was located on Washington Street, just a few blocks from where we were.

"Why a witch museum?" I inquired. "You don't think this has anything to do with witchcraft, do you?"

Harriet laughed. "No. Not at all, but the witch hunters were similar to the Mormons. They kept logs of people and families, much like a local census. If there are records dating back over fifty years, they'll have them. They are very thorough. Talk with Martha. She's the historian for the museum. I'll call her and let her know to expect you."

"What do you mean, very thorough?" I probed. "The witch hunts were over three hundred years ago. You don't still consider that kind of stuff around here, do you?"

Harriet's demeanor stiffened. "Old habits die hard, Mr.

Arnold," she said slowly. "There are those who still believe they walk among us." Harriet continued to give me an icy stare. After a moment of eye-to-eye contact, she regained her composure. "In this case, they will have the most accurate records if Mary's family is from Salem."

After getting directions, I began my walk to Washington Street. The shops in the area were filled with all forms of items from the past. In spite of the fact that most of the witch hunts and trials ended before 1750 in the United States, the memory of the craft was alive and well in Salem, Massachusetts.

I passed several interesting shops before reaching the museum. It stood on the corner of Washington and Church Street, aptly named because the Salem Witch Museum was actually in a former church. The building was ornate, with tall pillars at each edge of the front and a large stained-glass window in the upper center of the building between the columns. A chill ran through my body when I first saw it.

The outside temperature was in the high seventies. There was a noticeable difference between the cooler air inside the building.

Glancing around the museum, I saw the expected displays. A map of the witch-hunting sites on the wall, and portraits of the accused and executed, hung adjacent to the diagrams.

Several other visitors walked among the exhibitions, whispering and looking through historical ledgers. A small gift shop stood to my right, and to my left was an admissions counter.

"May I help you?"

The young woman who stood behind the counter had on a purple blouse, black pants, and a flowing black cloak. Her eyes were heavily made up and a large silver pentagram hung from a cord around her neck. When she smiled, I noticed her black lipstick. She had a name tag that read "Rebecca."

"Yes," I answered. "My name is Jason Arnold. I'm here to see Martha."

The smile broadened. "Welcome, Mr. Arnold, we've been expecting you," she said, extending a slender hand manicured with black fingernails.

I shook her hand, and following her lead, trailed her to the back of the museum. An almost invisible door was concealed in the back wall of the large room. Rebecca knocked softly.

"Yes?" came the reply.

Rebecca cracked the door and leaned through the opening.

"Martha, Mr. Arnold is here."

"Please, please, show him in," the voice said.

Rebecca opened the door wide, allowing me to gain entrance. The space doubled as an office and conference room. A woman in her mid-fifties, with short gray hair, sat behind a well-worn desk.

"Martha?" I asked.

The woman rose and walked around the desk to greet me.

"Yes. I'm Martha Corey-Bishop. Harriet said you'd be coming."

Rebecca had closed the door behind her and left us to talk.

I nodded. "Did she explain why I am here?"

"Very briefly," she said with a wave of her hand. "Please sit down."

We took seats on opposite sides of the small conference table. I laid my folder of information in front of me.

I couldn't help but notice that Martha was wearing an outfit similar to Rebecca's. She also wore a purple blouse with black pants, but had a smaller pentagram necklace.

I smiled. "Is the purple blouse part of a uniform here?" I inquired.

Martha didn't smile. "Obviously, you haven't done much research on witches, Mr. Arnold. These colorings and adornments are a strong part of our beliefs."

I was aghast. "You're a witch?" I blurted out.

Martha's stare mirrored the one that I had received from

Harriet. She said nothing for a moment, then glancing at the folder on the table, she asked, "How can I help you, Mr. Arnold?"

I spent the next half hour covering the events of my meeting with Mary and some of the things that had occurred since I rescued her off the plane, including Mary's inability to remember what city she was from and her astonishment at the technology which we took for granted. I conveyed Mary's story of her father, mother, and brother. Throughout the entire presentation, Martha's expression never changed. She sat staring and listening, her only movement being the occasional blinking of her crystal blue eyes.

When I finished my story, she took a deep breath and sighed.

"That's very interesting, Mr. Arnold. But why are you here? How do you think we can help you?"

I shrugged. "Not sure. I had to start somewhere. Christina Parker sent me to Harriet, and she sent me to you. I'm just trying to help this little girl find her home."

Martha had a questioning look on her face.

"Why did you choose to speak with Christina?"

"She has the same name as Mary's mother. I thought she might be a relative."

Martha burned a stare into my eyes. "Mary's last name is Parker?"

I nodded. "Yes. Does that make a difference?"

Martha's expression didn't change, but she blinked her eyes several times very quickly, indicating that something I said hit a nerve.

There was a moment of silence, during which we just looked at each other before she spoke.

"You said you had pictures."

I nodded. "Yes. Yes, I do—both before and after pictures."

I opened the folder and slid the pictures across the table. Martha first reached for the picture of Mary in her original dress, bringing it close to her eyes to see more clearly. As she looked at the photo, she slowly nodded, finally setting it back on the table and giving Mary's image in the more modern dress the same scrutiny.

"May I keep these for a while?" she asked. "I'd like to do a bit of research."

"Of course," I responded. "I'll be staying at the Salem Motel until the day after tomorrow. I leave at noon. Will I hear from you before then?"

"Yes. In fact, stop back and see me tomorrow afternoon at three. I may have some information for you by then."

CHAPTER 9

WHAT ARE THEY HIDING?

I walked back to retrieve my car and then drove to the Salem Motel. It was a single-story building with approximately twenty-five rooms. A bell jangled on the door as I entered the office. An attractive blonde woman, who appeared to be in her forties, walked out of a room in the back. She smiled.

"You must be Mr. Arnold."

"I am," I answered. "I have a reservation."

"Yes, you do," she said, pulling it up on the computer.

I slid my credit card across the counter. The clerk picked it up, examined it, and smiled, handing me the key to room twenty-two.

"I'm Alice. If you need anything, just call the front desk."

I nodded. "Thanks, I will."

I went back outside and found room twenty-two near the end of the building. It didn't appear as if anyone had registered in either room twenty-one or twenty-three, because there were no cars present and no lights on.

The room was a standard fare, low budget motel, a place to

shower and sleep. I picked up my phone and called Amy to give her an update and see how things were going at home.

She picked up before it barely finished its first ring.

"Jason."

"Yeah, honey. What's up?"

Amy sounded exasperated. "It's Mary."

"What's going on?" I asked.

The tone of Amy's voice caused me to hold my breath while I waited for her answer.

"Jason, she's different. I can't put a finger on it, but when she first got here, she seemed surprised by everything that happened. Now, she acts like she's been here all her life. Even Danielle noticed. She told Heather that she doesn't think you'll be able to find her parents."

"Why would she say that?"

"I don't know," Amy said. "She didn't seem extremely troubled by the idea."

"Well, just try to hang in there. I've got a bunch of people looking into her family history. Plus, I'm going to talk to the police department in a little while. Let's talk later tonight and I'll give you an update on what everyone has found."

Amy took my room number, the motel info, and hung up the phone.

I wondered if the police would be of any assistance. We had touched base with them earlier, and they appeared to be somewhat disinterested in helping. It appeared there were too many major crimes taking place in Salem. *Yeah, right,* I thought. An earlier impression came back to mind, so I decided to follow up on it.

"Good evening, Mr. Arnold."

"Please call me Jason," I said. "May I call you Alice?"

"Of course," the motel clerk answered. "How can I help you?"

I explained my reasoning for being in Salem, and what steps I had taken since I had been there. Alice listened intently.

"So, you think the girl is a witch?" she asked.

"A witch?" I stuttered. "Why does everyone think in witch terms here?"

Alice laughed. "It comes quite naturally. You are in the witch capital of the country, you know. Many people still practice the craft, though only a few do so publicly. I simply assumed since you went to the museum, you may have thought the girl was a witch."

I explained the theory of the witch's population recording. After a moment, Alice smiled.

"I know just the person. Salem is a closed town, Mr. Arnold —uh, Jason. Those that are truly in the know don't take to outsiders prying into our business. It's safer that way."

The tone of Alice's voice caused me to ask an obvious question.

"Do you practice witchcraft?"

"Some questions are better left unanswered. Let's just say that I have a solid working knowledge of the principles and practices of the craft."

I was quick to reply. "Alice, I have no negative connotations about witches, Wiccans, Pagans, or anything else. I've never had an occasion to deal with any of them before now, but I've always been intrigued by things that fall outside the lines of normalcy. Also, I figure that what a person chooses to do with their life is their own business. All I want to do is find this little girl's family."

"I understand," she answered with a smile. "Norma can help you if anyone can."

I took the address and the brief directions which Alice had written on a motel notepad, and headed to the car.

After a ten-minute ride, I turned onto Jackson Road and searched for Norma's address. Her house was near the outskirts of town on a street that looked very much like my own neighborhood in Michigan. I was able to read her address easily from the street. I parked near the curb and walked to the small porch of the ranch-style home. A pentagram knocker hung at the ready as I searched for the doorbell. Before I pushed the button, the inside door opened from behind.

A woman of approximately sixty years of age smiled at me as she pushed the screen open.

"You must be Jason," she said.

I smiled. "Guilty as charged. Are you Norma?"

We exchanged brief pleasantries as she led the way into a well-lit kitchenette. She pulled a chair away from the small dining table and walked to a full coffeepot sitting on the counter.

"Coffee?" she asked.

"Yes, thank you. Just a little cream, please."

Norma was obviously a no-frills person. The decor of the house was simple and appeared to be missing an old world charm.

Norma set my coffee in front of me and pulled out a chair at the opposite end of the table, taking her own seat.

"Alice said you could use some help," she said over the brim of her mug.

I nodded. "That's right. I'm trying to find the parents of a young girl that I pulled off the plane that crashed recently in Toronto. Perhaps you saw it on the news."

Norma smiled with a nod. "I did. A miracle, that one. Hard to believe no one died."

The short gray-haired woman took another drink of her coffee and sat the mug on the table, then turned to look out her large kitchen window.

"Why did you become involved, Jason?" she asked without looking at me.

I was confused. "What do you mean? Someone had to help her. The authorities didn't have a clue what to do, and I have three girls of my own. I just figured someone needed to do something, so I did."

Norma nodded, still not looking in my direction. After a few moments of silence during which she continued to stare out the window, she slowly turned to look at me. Her eyes burned into my own.

"Jason, I think you're a wonderful and gallant man. If the situation were different ..." her voice trailed off, she shook her head slightly and continued, "but, it's not. Your help may have actually complicated things."

"What do you mean, complicated things?" I asked. "How could my help complicate anything?"

Norma smiled again, reaching over to place her hand on top of mine, patting it lightly before resting it.

"Our world is a very complex place. Many of its inhabitants walk around with their heads in the sand, unaware that what they believe is only a fantasy. Others of us deal with reality. Sometimes that makes the world a more comfortable place to be. Your help has crossed the line between fantasy and reality. Very soon, that line will be uncrossed and your life will return to normal."

I was more confused than before, and now I was becoming angry.

"Norma, Alice said you could help me. I don't have a clue what the heck you're talking about, and I'm certainly no closer to finding Mary's parents than I was when I got here." I slid my chair back and stood to leave. "Are you going to help me or not?"

The older woman didn't move a muscle. If anything, her stare became more direct. She pointed to the chair.

"Please sit down, Mr. Arnold."

The change in Norma's attitude was obvious. I reluctantly resumed my seat. Norma took a deep breath, and without taking her eyes off of mine, spoke calmly.

"Mary's situation is unique. She did not board the plane in Boston, and you will not be able to find her parents. What you will do, if you continue to ask questions, is stir up a great deal of controversy and aggravate energies that do not need disturbing."

I returned Norma's stare, nodding slightly as I did. I had obviously stepped into some place where I wasn't welcome.

"If she didn't get on the plane in Boston, where did she get on?"

Norma's face softened a little.

"Your questions are valid, Mr. Arnold. However, there are no answers that would satisfy your curiosity. Might I suggest you get a good night's sleep and return to Detroit in the morning?"

"You can suggest anything you want, Norma, but I'm not going anywhere until I find Mary's parents. I will do that with, or without, your help."

I again slid my chair back and stood up, this time taking a step toward the door. Before I reached for the knob to let myself out, I turned back to look at Norma. She stood in the kitchen entryway with her hands on her hips, watching me.

"If she didn't get on the plane in Boston," I repeated, "when did she get on?"

Norma smiled. "Sometime after you began your final approach to Toronto. I'd say somewhere near Guelph, Ontario, if you must know. Blessed be, Mr. Arnold."

I stared at the smiling woman for a moment and then stepped into the sunshine, pulling the door closed behind me, the pentagram door knocker softly tapping as I did.

Logically, what Norma had said wasn't possible. I was beginning to think that all the people in Salem were hiding something. There certainly seemed to be many who were into witchcraft, so I concluded it was a subject I needed a crash course in. I headed back to town and the Salem Witch Museum.

The young woman who stood behind the receptionist's

counter wore a name tag which read Nicole. She was dressed like Rebecca, in a purple blouse, black pants, and a pentagram necklace. Unlike Rebecca, Nicole wasn't wearing a cape.

"Mr. Arnold," she said with a smile, "you're back."

Her recognition caught me off guard. I hadn't met her earlier when I was at the museum. Obviously, my name had been passed among the staff.

"Yes," I answered, "I am. When I was here earlier, I noticed some books in the gift shop. Do you know if you carry any basic books on the craft?"

Nicole smiled. "Of course. We have one for beginners called *Wicca and Witchcraft for Dummies*. Don't take the title insultingly. Most people know very little about our beliefs. This book will answer a great many questions for you."

CHAPTER 10

THE RUNAROUND

My stay in the museum was brief, and soon I was headed back to the Salem Motel.

They patterned the manual after many of the how-to books that had to do with computer operations. The information was carefully categorized and simply written. At least after an hour or two with this book, I'd hope to have some idea of what was going on in Salem, Massachusetts.

I parked in front of my room and unlocked the door. Just before I entered, I had an idea. I walked down to the office. Alice was waiting as I closed the door behind me.

"Enjoy your visit?" she asked.

"Uh, no, not really," I answered. "I thought you said Norma would be able to help me."

"She did, Mr. Arnold. She gave you some very sound advice. Unfortunately, it doesn't seem as though you're going to take it."

I took a deep sigh and looked away from Alice for a minute, thinking. When I turned back to look at her, she was still smiling.

"Who are you people? I mean, is everyone in this town a witch?"

Alice laughed. "No. There are still a few holdouts, but we're working on them. They'll eventually come around."

"And, Norma?" I asked.

"Norma is our High Priestess. She's the leader of our coven."

"Coven?" I said. "I didn't think they had those anymore."

"Yes, we do. You'll find out more when you read your book," she answered with a smile. "The Silver Broom Coven is one of the oldest in Salem."

I hadn't taken the book to the office with me. How did she know I bought it? It appeared everyone in town was aware of my presence and my actions. I was starting to feel very uncomfortable.

"Why won't you let me help this little girl? Why can't I get a straight answer from anybody?"

"I think Norma said it best. No help is needed. Everything will work out according to schedule, provided you don't interfere."

I was confused by a couple of key points. Since when is saving someone's life interference? If it was, I could have saved myself a great deal of trouble by leaving her on the plane. Was she supposed to die? What about Norma's statement that Mary had boarded the plane over Guelph? Was this some kind of sci-fi thriller? It didn't fit. Our world was real. Things like that didn't happen. Norma had mentioned fantasy and reality. Which one was this?

Alice smiled. I nodded in understanding. Without saying another word, I turned and headed for the door. As I pushed the door open to leave, Alice added, "Blessed be, Mr. Arnold. Blessed be."

I stopped for a moment before exiting, nodded, and then walked out the door. Blessed be, my ass.

The book was just as I had perceived—well organized and easy to read. As I skimmed through, I learned that the dark side of witchcraft was extremely overplayed by today's society.

Modern witchcraft is based on the practice of Wicca. Witches of today are basically positive oriented and earth-centered. The rituals which they perform are done to honor the earth and its seasons, and to bring respect to their Father-Mother images. These are the masculine and feminine energies of their lives. The casting of evil curses is a thing of the past. Yet, if this theory is true, why were they so opposed to my being here?

It appeared Alice sincerely wanted to help. Now that I had a better understanding of the craft, I felt less defensive and thought that she might fill in a few of the missing pieces I had about Mary's case. It was past my usual time for supper, but I stopped at the office on my way to eat. A short blonde woman stood behind the counter.

"May I help you?" she asked.

"Yes, I'm Jason Arnold in room 22. Is Alice still around?"

The young woman looked puzzled.

"Alice who?" she asked.

"Alice," I repeated, "the other receptionist. She was here earlier."

"Sorry, Mr. Arnold. I don't know an Alice. I've been here since noon. My name is Elizabeth. Is there anything I can help you with?"

A very sick feeling came over me. "She was here just a couple of hours ago. I talked to her. She checked me in."

Elizabeth pulled my registration card and examined it.

"No, Mr. Arnold. Eugene checked you in. He's our night manager. I replaced him when I came in at noon."

"Perhaps I have the name wrong," I said. "She's tall with black hair ..."

Elizabeth smiled and shook her head. "I'm sorry, Mr. Arnold. There's no one working here with that description."

My earlier fears were escalating. Alice was wearing a tag with her name and the logo of the motel on it. I wasn't mistaken. I was being railroaded.

The Museum Café was less than a block from the motel and had a menu of home-cooked delicacies. I opted for the chicken and dumplings, and a bowl of navy bean soup.

The food was as good as my mother used to make, and she was a great cook. A large slice of Dutch apple pie, a la mode, completed the sumptuous meal.

I'd given a lot of thought to the day's activities. Everyone seemed willing to help, but instead, they led me on one wild-goose chase after another. I'd spent the better part of the day here and accomplished virtually nothing.

I wanted to call home and get some sleep. If no one would help me, I might as well be in Detroit. At least I'd be with my family.

Amy answered the phone on the second ring. "Jason, I'm so glad it's you. Have you found out anything?"

"No, honey, I'm being given the runaround. Everybody knows I'm coming wherever I go, and they have encouraged me to quit searching and go home. I'm going to stop at the library in the morning and then come home tomorrow evening. I think there's a flight that leaves here around four. How are things there?"

Amy whispered, "Hold on." I heard her walking, then close a door. She spoke in low tones. "Mary is growing."

"What's that supposed to mean?" I asked.

"Just what I said. She's bigger than Danielle. I had to give her one of my sweatshirts this morning. Something weird is going on. The girls are scared to death, and even the dog looks at her funny."

My first reaction was to tell Amy that she was imagining things. After what I had been through today, I was certain what she was seeing was actually happening.

"Just keep her out of the limelight. I'll be home tomorrow. Everyone here says we are interfering with a plan, but I'm hoping I can find out more at the library. When I make my flight arrangements, I'll call you."

I called the airlines and booked a seat on a non-stop flight from Boston to Detroit that left at 3:45 p.m. That would put me home at about 8:00.

Waking to a day of bright sunshine after a restless sleep brightened my spirits. I refreshed myself with a hot shower and suffered through a cup of in-room coffee before dressing and heading back to the Museum Café. I was looking forward to breakfast.

Bridget greeted me at my booth almost as soon as I sat down. I ordered coffee and orange juice and looked at the menu. Like their dinners, the breakfasts at the Museum Café looked generous in size. I ordered ham and eggs. While I waited for my food, I stirred the condiments into my coffee and savored the taste of fresh-brewed Columbian roast.

My thoughts returned to the meetings and conversations which had taken place the day before. Rationally, I had to conclude that I was in the heart of witch country, if there was such a thing. I surmised that if I were in the southern part of the eastern United States, most people I spoke with would profess opposite ideologies. For now, I was stuck with Mary and witchcraft.

"Aren't you Mr. Arnold?"

Bridget was back.

"Yes. Yes, I am. How did you know?"

Bridget smiled. "I don't mean to seem nosey, Mr. Arnold, but everyone in Salem knows you're here and why you're here. Personally, I think what you're doing is very nice. I understand. I went through what Mary is going through right now. She'll be fine."

I was totally taken aback by Bridget's statements and asked, "How does everyone know who I am, and what exactly is Mary going through?"

"Would you like more coffee, Mr. Arnold?" She asked with a smile.

We stared eye-to-eye for a moment. "Yes, please."

Bridget left to get my refill. Man, I felt like I was in a deep fishbowl. Had they monitored my phone conversations? The thought of going home and passing the responsibility of Mary's future on to someone else was growing in my mind. What had I gotten myself into?

Bridget was back with the coffee and my food. As I had expected, it was a wonderful serving of breakfast favorites. When at last my cup was full, Bridget placed my bill face down on the table. On top was a small slip of paper with a name on it.

"See this lady at the Salem College Library. She'll fill you in on some details. Then stop back for lunch if you have questions. Blessed be, Mr. Arnold."

Blessed be, indeed! Bridget went to service another table, and I folded the slip of paper and put it in my pocket.

The name on the slip was Thelma Hansen. Who she was or what she knew, I didn't know, but I was certainly headed to the Salem College Library to find out.

Unlike the large Midwestern universities, whose campuses are spread over vast areas, Salem College was compact. The entire facility was contained in a single, two block area. I parked near the library door and walked inside.

Libraries have a unique smell to them. The aging books render an acidic aroma that seems to have a historical flavor to it.

A young woman stood behind the check-out counter sorting through some books which had been returned. When I reached the counter, she looked up and smiled.

"May I help you?"

"Yes, I'm looking for Thelma Hansen."

"Of course. You must be Mr. Arnold. She's expecting you. Please follow me."

Once again, a feeling of vulnerability swept over me. *Well, at least I'm famous in Salem, Massachusetts*, I thought.

I followed the young woman down a long-tiled hallway. We entered the main room and walked back to a large corner office. It was well appointed and obviously belonged to someone in authority.

"Thelma, this is Mr. Arnold."

The middle-aged woman smiled and stood up behind her desk to shake my hand.

"Thank you, Katie. Would you like some coffee, Mr. Arnold?"

"Uh, no, thank you. I just finished breakfast."

"Very well. Katie, tell Sharon to hold my calls while I'm in this meeting."

The young woman turned and went to do Thelma's bidding.

"You're quite a celebrity, Mr. Arnold," she began.

I smiled with a nod. "So it seems. How does everyone know I'm coming, no matter where I go?"

"Salem is like that. Many people come here who don't understand our culture. They're more interested in disrupting than helping. Your acclaim seems to be more positive, if that's possible."

"I hope that's a good thing," I said.

"Oh, it is. It is. We really are trying to help you understand. Most of us appreciate what you're trying to do, but as you've been told, there is no need for help. Everything is on schedule."

CHAPTER 11
ANSWERS

I noticed Thelma was wearing a cross necklace. "You're not Witch?" I asked.

She shook her head. "No, but I understand the craft and the things they have to go through. They are highly misunderstood. Personally, I think they're a bit misguided, but that's only because I was raised as a Christian. Here, we try to get along. I don't judge them and they don't judge me. Our mutual respect seems to work well."

"Are you familiar with my purpose for being here?"

Thelma nodded, her straight, shoulder-length hair bobbing as she did.

"Yes, of course. Since you are not Wiccan, they have elected me to be their spokesperson."

I was virtually holding my breath as she moved a few papers from the center to the side of her desk.

"Jason, I know you have read a book on the basic witchcraft information. There is so much that you don't know. It started in 1692. The daughter and niece of a prominent minister became ill. When they didn't respond to medical treatment, the doctor suggested that they had been bewitched and therefore were suffering from demonic possession. In spring of that year, the Salem Witch Trials began. They accused over two hundred people of witchcraft. Before sanity returned, nineteen people were hanged for being witches. In truth, none of them were guilty of any crime."

I was vaguely familiar with the history of the witch trials, but never understood what had started them, or when they ended.

"So, what does that have to do with Mary?" I asked. "This is present day, not 1692."

Thelma smiled. "How right you are, but time is, let's just say, fluid. Really, 1692 was not that long ago."

I repeated my question. "What does this have to do with Mary?"

Thelma swiveled in her chair for a minute, staring at me. After a moment's reflection, she squared herself up to her desk and rolled forward, resting her elbows on top.

"I think it's time for a history lesson. Please hold any questions until I have finished."

I nodded in agreement.

"Fortunately, Gallows Hill, where the witches were hanged, is an extremely powerful place. Earth's energy is magnified there. Also, the population of witches in the area was very large, much bigger than the courts could have perceived."

I sat and listened for nearly an hour, occasionally shaking my head. What Thelma was talking about wasn't possible.

"And you expect me to believe that?"

"Believe it or don't, Jason. That's your prerogative. Whether or not you believe, it is true. When you stop back at the café for lunch, Bridget will confirm what I have said." Thelma stood up behind her desk, indicating that our meeting was finished. "Have a good day, Mr. Arnold."

The formality of her closure said that we were done talking. I nodded, shook her hand, and found my way out. When I reached the main area of the library, I realized it would be a good time to do a little research on my own.

Katie was still behind the checkout counter.

"Is there someplace I can use a computer?"

She smiled, "Sure, Mr. Arnold, use any computer in the information center." She pointed toward a glassed-in room to my right. "Just hit enter on the keyboard and the sign-in screen will come up."

I entered Salem witches into the search field. Nearly four hundred thousand sites came up. I spent the next two hours reading through some of them. By the time I had closed the links, I had become a veritable expert on the Salem Witch Trials. How were these things possible?

It was now lunchtime, and I was curious to see what Bridget would have to say. I got into my car and drove to the Museum Café.

Bridget sat waiting in a corner booth when I entered. She smiled and waved me over. I slid in across from her.

"Not working?" I asked.

"No. I got off at eleven. I let other people fight the lunch crowd," she answered with a laugh. "Did you talk with Thelma?"

"Yeah, I did. I also spent some time online doing research."

Abby walked to our booth. "You guys want something to drink?"

We placed an order for soft drinks and the waitress left. When she was out of earshot, Bridget continued, "So, now you understand?"

I shook my head. "I'm not so sure. What Thelma told me is a little hard to swallow. In fact, it's unbelievable."

Bridget's face became solemn. "Believe it, Jason. It's the truth. If not for the craft, none of us would be here."

"Can you prove that?"

Bridget pulled the upper part of her blouse to the side. "Ever see one of these?"

For the moment, I just stared speechless.

Just below her collarbone was a small tattoo. It was the image of a black letter "W" with a Christian cross over it, done in red ink.

I thought of Mary's tattoo. "Where did you get that?" I asked.

"We all have them." She then pulled up her left sleeve to a point near the top of her shoulder. "And these," she added with finality.

Branded into the skin of her upper shoulder was a pentagram. It was approximately three inches across and raised a large welt of scar tissue that was easily visible.

I stared at the brand. "Why?"

"People are afraid of things they don't understand," she said. "When they can't explain the reasons why things happen, their only answer is to strike out at them. Witchcraft was an easy target."

We ate lunch and talked. Mostly about events which were more recent. Witchcraft was alive and well and practiced by many people in the area. An understanding replaced the fear that was once raised at the thought of people being witches. Visitors to Salem were unaware that witches ran most of the businesses, taught in all the schools, and held most of the political positions in the city. Things had come a long way.

My return flight to Detroit was uneventful. I was eager to see Amy, the girls, and Mary. The fact that I now understood the circumstances surrounding Mary and her survival, our participation, became a unique event. I hurried from the airport to my home.

After the normal hugs and kisses, Amy stepped back from me and furrowed her brow.

"You look whipped," she said.

I nodded, "I am. At least I know we're not all losing our minds. Where's Mary?"

"She's upstairs. What do you mean, we aren't losing our minds? I think I'm losing my mind."

I laughed. "No, honey, you're sane. I'd just like everyone to be here before I explain what I've found out. You may find it hard to believe, but from all the people I've talked to, I think it's the truth. We'll certainly find out soon enough."

It took a few minutes to get everyone together. I suggested that they all get refreshments. Mary was noticeably missing.

"Where's Mary?"

"She's coming," Amy said with a nervous chuckle. "You're going to need an incredible story to answer this one."

We were all sitting in the den when Mary came in. When I saw her, I couldn't believe my eyes. The nine-year-old girl that I had pulled off the plane had transformed into a beautiful young woman. She had matured physically and was now as tall as Amy. She smiled when she saw me, finally walking to an over-stuffed chair and taking a seat.

"I've met some of your friends," I began.

Mary nodded. "Yes, I had a feeling. I'm sorry I didn't remember. I could have saved you a great deal of effort."

I chuckled. "It's been a wild goose chase, but I understand. I think you'll be happy to know how many friends you really have, but you should know what transpired. I'm sure you'll find it amusing."

She replied, "Anything you can offer would be helpful."

"Everything started when I went to Christina Parker's house in Salem. She seemed very sincere and wanted to help. She sent me to another lady, who referred me to a different woman, who in turn recommended I talk to someone at the library named Thelma. It was obvious everyone was trying to confuse me, hoping I'd simply get frustrated and leave, but Thelma offered a detailed explanation regarding the events we've experienced and why. When I finally spoke with a waitress named Bridget earlier today, she confirmed Thelma's story and helped me sort things out. Mary, can you show me your shoulder?"

Mary raised the sleeve of her blouse. In exactly the same spot, as it appeared on Bridget's shoulder, was the brand of a pentagram. I presumed the tattoo which the girls saw on her upper chest would also be the same as the one on Bridget.

My explanation had progressed to the point where I was describing the events which took place at Norma's house when the door-bell rang. Amy walked over to answer it.

I could hear introductions taking place and, in only a moment, Amy returned to the den with two visitors.

It was Sarah Good and Henri LeBeau. I walked around the coffee table and shook hands with both of them.

"Welcome, they told me you'd be coming. Please, have a seat," I invited.

They both looked at Mary. I nodded.

Henri began, "For the moment, we're Mary's foster parents. In a short time, she will assimilate into present day society and develop her own life. Until then, she needs to be with us."

I understood their intent, but Mary was as safe with us as with anyone. I turned to Henri.

"Henri, why can't she just stay here with us?"

The tall man smiled. "The reason will be obvious, but before I get into that, I would like to set the record straight on something and apologize for all the confusion. My name is not Henri. I'm really Giles Corey. You may have read about me in your research. I was pressed to death as my punishment on September 19, 1692. Mary's execution was a few days later at Gallows Hill. Our friend Sarah was punished first, in July. Only because of the craft and an organized effort by the covens, are we here today to talk about it."

"Why can't we help Mary adapt?"

Giles laughed. "And you'll be able to explain to your friend Larry, the police officer, how the nine-year-old girl you pulled off the plane is actually an adult in only three days?" He shook his head. "It wouldn't work, Jason. The media would be all over it. Mary would be taken into custody and vigorously assaulted with tests, examinations, and detailed questioning. After all she's been through, I'm sure you wouldn't want to subject her to that. It'll be better to tell everyone Mary's parents showed up and took her, and that they requested complete anonymity. Once we've left your home, no one will be able to find us, and Mary will be safe to live the life she deserves."

The look on Amy and the girl's faces was still one of confusion. I'd been unable to get to the good part of the explanation.

"Could someone please tell me what's going on?" Amy demanded.

There was a moment of uncomfortable silence before Giles finally spoke again. "A good number of us were wrongfully executed for practicing witchcraft, but now that same mysterious energy gives us all a second chance at life."

Sarah added, "The Salem Witch Trials were a gross injustice. At the time they occurred, those who followed the Wiccan ideologies did so in fear and without public displays of expression. Once the trials actually began taking place, those in the craft decided they needed a way to rescue the people who were going to be punished. The local covens banded together to create rituals and a powerful incantation which would remove the soul of the person being executed, moving it through time, to a period when the craft was more accepted. Their physical bodies would be recreated, and since things have progressed enough, now is the right time. Many of those who were saved landed in Salem. Mary is one of the last to be rescued and restored."

Giles interjected, "I think it's time we let the Arnolds get on with their lives. We've caused enough confusion and uncertainty."

The three of them rose together. We all followed suit.

Sarah walked over, gave us a hug, and reassured Amy that everything was as it should be.

"We can't thank you enough for all that you've done." Sarah reached her hands out to the girls. "And to you, young ladies, your parents should be very proud of you."

Mary stepped forward and hugged the girls. "I'll never forget any of you."

Giles and I shook hands. "Please take good care of her," I said. "She's kinda special to us."

Giles nodded. "She's in good hands, thanks to all of you. Perhaps our paths will cross again one day."

Mary finished giving hugs all around, ending with a tight squeeze of my neck.

"Thank you, Mr. Arnold."

We stared eye-to-eye for a moment and then we both nodded before walking in silence to the front door. As they exited, Giles turned to face us before descending the front steps.

"Blessed be, to you and your family, Jason Arnold."

"And blessed be to all of you," I replied, closing the door behind them.

Amy stared at me as though someone had just told her the Easter Bunny was real.

"Is this even possible?"

I shrugged. "Heck, I don't know. It's either possible or someone has an incredible sense of humor. From what I can see, there are far too many people involved for it to be a joke. Besides, how do you get a nine-year-old girl to become an adult in only three days? We all saw it happen. That part was real."

Amy responded, "You can't deny what you see with your own eyes."

"I asked Bridget why they didn't just have Mary show up in

Salem like the others, but she didn't know the answer to that. It's likely the same questions would have arisen there. If all had gone well, the plane we were on would have simply landed in Toronto. Mary would have walked off to be greeted by Giles and Sarah. They would have disappeared into the night to a safe house where Mary could have completed her transition phase. When the plane crashed, it changed everything. Bridget told me the powers-that-be discussed the situation and decided on a new plan with me bringing Mary home. In retrospect, it sounds somewhat reasonable."

"Do you really think it's true?" Amy asked.

"I don't know, honey. What I was told in Salem matches what appears to have taken place. The arrival of Giles and Sarah today is what they said would happen. The reincarnation spell created by the ancient covens seems to be working, and is bringing the executed witches back to life in our time. I don't know how it can be real, but I do believe it's true."

The girls all looked at me like I had lost my mind.

"What do you guys think?" I asked.

They shrugged simultaneously and shook their heads.

"Dad," Danielle began, "we're glad you're home." She looked at her sisters and then back at me. "We're happy we could help, but could we order pizza? We're starving and the Red Wings are on TV tonight."

Boy, was I glad to be home.

Thank you for reading *Mary*. We hope you enjoyed it! If you'd like to continue The Starlite Supernatural Mystery Series, you can read our standalone shorts in any order.

AUTHOR NOTES

Thank you for reading our story.
We love hearing your feedback, so we hope you'll post a review.

If you liked *Mary*, please check out our other
Starlite Supernatural Mysteries.

Receive an exciting look into *1421 Maple* by signing up for our
newsletter using the Bookfunnel link below.
https://dl.bookfunnel.com/xpkhinq30n

Plus, get behind the scenes tidbits and learn about new releases.

1421 Maple

"This is a great short story read. It is fast paced and enjoyable. I
didn't see the ending coming, and honestly it's probably because
I don't read these types of books normally. I absolutely loved
the relationship between Jimmy and his dad; it was a nice to see
a strong father son relationship. I also really enjoyed how

genuine the author's were in writing about Jimmy's reaction to the lot being built upon. If you like paranormal reads, then you'll definitely like this short story – and you'll be able to read it in under an hour!"
- Kristin G.

1421 Maple

"I really enjoyed this short story! It's one of those thrillers that you can finish on a lunch break and feel like you spent 45 minutes in an alternate universe. I was intrigued from the beginning, but a plot twist came around and I had to keep reading to see what was going on. Perfect for those just getting into a thriller genre!"
- Brenna P., Outreach Librarian

ALSO BY RAY & MICHELE

If you enjoyed this Starlite Mystery, check out our other unique spellbinding shorts. They're the perfect escape when you're pressed for time.

The Starlite Supernatural Mystery Series:

Haunted

The Wind

The Promise

Mary

1421 Maple

Sarah

Coming Soon

Enter the web of intrigue, suspense, and danger in

The Sean Thomas Paranormal Mystery Series

Book 1 - *A Switch in Time*

For a complete list of Ray and Michele's books, visit

www.rayandmichelefraser.com

https://books2read.com/MicheleFraser

ABOUT THE AUTHORS

Ray and Michele are a full-time writing team with a serious passion for storytelling. They combine their love of writing, vivid imagination, and years of experience as professional spirit mediums to guide their readers into uncharted territories.

In 1994, Ray's intuitions fostered by Cherokee and Scottish ancestry, led him to open Mystiques-West Metaphysical Center in Michigan. During the twenty-three years of operation, Ray hosted a #1 radio talk show and a live TV show, called *The Mystical Connection*. They performed home cleansing, organized ghost hunts, taught classes in mediumship, and led weekly public seances to connect clients to their departed loved ones on the other side. The messages from spirit have helped many to find peace. Ray also facilitated the last four National Houdini Seances sponsored by Houdini historian Sid Radner.

In addition to readings and life coaching sessions, Ray's work as an ordained minister has provided his clientele with years of grief and relationship counseling, weddings, and funerals.

As a screenwriter, Michele brings her love of film into the fold by incorporating her own style of creativity into their endeavors. She's also the backbone of the editing process, social media management, cover design, and marketing.

Ray and Michele infuse their stories with mystery, intrigue, tales of the afterlife, and other worldly phenomena to create a fascinating and adventurous journey for readers.

For more info - linktr.ee/RayandMicheleFraser

Ray's extensive background and keen storytelling abilities combined with Michele's love of screenwriting and editing has made them a powerhouse duo.
www.rayandmichelefraser.com

DON'T MISS OUT

Signed paperbacks
can be easily requested via our website.
www.rayandmichelefraser.com

Click the button below to sign up for our fan exclusive
newsletter to get behind the scenes tidbits and learn about new
book releases.

There's no charge or obligation and we never sell your
information.

https://rayandmichelefraser.com/newsletter

BOOKS 2 READ

https://books2read.com/MicheleFraser

WHAT PEOPLE ARE SAYING

Haunted

"Ray and Michele do not disappoint. I could not put this book down. It left me wanting to know more. I'm a big fan of haunted houses and was very intrigued with this story. I honestly didn't see the story going the way it did. I actually felt as if I was there. I felt all the emotions the characters felt. I'm still in awe at the story and cannot wait until their next book!!"
- Shana L.

The Wind

"This book ensnared me from the get-go. Like the wind whispering encouragement to keep on reading. The fact that the writers are able to create such a wonderfully thrilling story within such few pages is pure magic. It kept me on my toes and I read the whole thing in one sitting. I genuinely believe this could be adapted into a full length novel.

Character development was great especially for a novella and the storyline was stella.

I would highly recommend this, and during the start it was giving me major Phantom vibes by Dean R Koontz and he is one of my all time favs in the thriller department.

If you like thrillers, or wives tales or simply short stories then this is the book for you, even if you only said yes to one of those."
- Juniper Raven

The Promise

"Just finished reading this story... and I am blessed beyond words! It's a beautiful paranormal novella focusing on grief, loss, sadness, and ultimately - redemption. For lovers of *Chicken Soup for the Soul* books and the *Sixth Sense* film, you will be delighted to have the time to read this short story - and feel compelled to engage in the entire series! Thank you to @rayandmichelefraser for the wonderful opportunity to share this story of mystery and intrigue with you all! I highly recommend and rate it 5 of 5 sweet stars!"

\- Deb

1421 Maple

"I really enjoyed this short story! It's one of those thrillers that you can finish on a lunch break and feel like you spent 45 minutes in an alternate universe. I was intrigued from the beginning, but a plot twist came around and I had to keep reading to see what was going on. Perfect for those just getting into a thriller genre!"

\- Brenna P., Outreach Librarian

Sarah

"This is a page turner. Sarah finds herself in a destructive marriage that is not at all what she thought she was getting into. Charlie is charming on the outside with an evil heart. To survive, she had to do something drastic. But will she ever be truly free from her torturing husband? Fans of A Tell Tale Heart will find this an interesting twist on a classic story."

\- Brook